About the Author

For Anastasia, who wrote and published her first short novel titled "New Beginnings" aged 10-11, writing has been a lifelong passion. Her second published work "A Sure Sign of a Witch", written around the age of 15, marks a serious step forward and establishes her progression since childhood. As a Romanian immigrant, she is proud to call herself a budding author writing in the English language and she hopes for many successes to come.

Contents

A SURE SIGN OF A WITCH

By

Anastasia-Elena S.M

A Sure Sign of A Witch

Author: Anastasia-Elena S.M

ISBN 978-1-83538-708-5 (Paperback)
     978-1-83538-709-2 (E-Book)

Book Cover design and Layout by:
    Maple Publishers
    www.maplepublishers.com

Published by:
    Maple Publishers
    Fairbourne Drive, Atterbury,
    Milton Keynes,
    MK10 9RG, UK
    www.maplepublishers.com

A CIP catalogue record for this title is available from the British Library.

Part 2

Part 3

Acknowledgments

I would firstly like to thank my father, whose financial contribution made publication possible. I would also like to thank my friend and mentor, Dr Johnson, who patiently read my work and made thoughtful suggestions, and without whose encouragements the book would not have progressed 😊.

My family, including my mother and step-father, provided me with invaluable support throughout my writing process. My mother, who has always believed in me and in my creativity, and who was the backbone in the project, deserves as much credit for the completion of the book as me. If my mother hadn't pushed me to keep going and keep growing, the novel would be nothing more than a vague story idea, undeveloped and unfinished. Instead, thanks to my mother's help, I can proudly call myself an author.

Part 1

1

Bea

A crow caws grumpily and hops away, his body a flurry of ruffled black satin feathers. I watch from behind a foggy window, wringing my hands, my heart fluttering. It's early; the clouds, tinted grey, envelope the weak rays of dilute sunlight, and their moisture seeps into the air, weighing it down like a wet blanket.

Our graveyard of a front garden is littered with crawling weeds and ominous thorn bushes and shivering foxgloves and serpentine limbs of blackberry plant. I open the window, and a brisk draught leaks inside. My arms are bare, and the skin prickles and I tremble, but I keep the window open. The air smells fresh and sweet, and inside it's musty and stuffy and sour.

Everything is still. I can hear my own ragged breathing and the croaking calls of birds outside, but apart from this, the street is silent.

And I'm alone.

2

Janine

Green blurs outside zoom past as the train rattles along the line. My suitcase knocks against my knees. A fly buzzes past my ear. I flinch.

"How much further?" I ask. Mum sighs and flicks the page of her magazine, ever cool and calm.

"Just a bit, Janine," she says without looking up.

Even this past week, when her temper has been tried endlessly, no doubt, she's remained remarkably collected. She seems distracted, though, and agitated: I know that she isn't really reading the magazine; her eyes are fixed on the page, but her mind is racing excitedly.

I kick my legs against my seat, bored and sleepy.

"Are we almost there?"

Mum doesn't reply at all this time. I'm not sure if she even heard me. I don't ask her again.

I think back to last week, when Mum got the phone call from the solicitor about her uncle Casper. It was an explosive morning. Everything was upside down. Mum was hysterically happy to hear about her uncle's death. She never really knew him anyway, she said. He was her last living family, and he left us his entire estate and quite a bit of cash, at least by our standards. She was in such a rush to sort everything out. My mum had never been so organised. She was making calls left and right, stirring her cup of tea with one hand and viciously scribbling out letters with the other. The landlord, who Mum had always sort of trembled around because she tended to pay the rent a bit late sometimes, had no choice but to be persuaded to make do with the one week notice we'd given him. It was all happening so quickly.

Mum was absolutely thrilled to be leaving our flat. She used to say it sucked all the money out of her, even though it was a rubbish, dumpy, dingy old thing. The flat was a suffocated little place, with dark damp spots on the walls and ragged, grubby carpets that smelled faintly of urine no matter how much Mum scrubbed. Mum said she chose it because it was close to my school, so I wouldn't have to take a bus or train. It wasn't worth it. My school wasn't all that great either.

I think it also sucked the life out of her. She was so sick of it all. She'd come home from her cleaning job, absolutely exhausted, and almost collapse on the workload that awaited her back at the flat. There was always something that needed fixing, like a wonky window or a lock that didn't actually lock properly, and if Mum couldn't sort it out herself, she'd need to go grovelling to the landlord. If it wasn't that, it was the endless bills. She never told me, but I saw her pinched eyebrows and tight lips when the dreaded envelopes came and she was anxious that we couldn't make rent, or the phone bill, or the electric. Our television was still on the counter in the kitchen, but we hadn't been able to watch anything for months because Mum couldn't afford it anymore and it just sat plonked there, gathering dust. I heard her on the phone to people, begging for loans. She always said she'd pay them back, but I don't think she ever really did.

Great-Uncle Casper's house is in the Cotswolds. That's where we're headed now. I feel quite conflicted about it. I don't really know *how* to react. Leafy fields and quiet open spaces aren't really my thing, and I think Mum is a bit nervous about this green new beginning in the countryside too, but she insisted that it would be quick, like tearing off a plaster. She seems unsure, but she's far too consumed by the thought of an idyllic, almost unbelievable opportunity to start afresh. I know it'll make her happy, regardless of if it's easy or not.

The train halts. Mum, who had just sunken into a light sleep, snaps her eyes open sharply and she's instantly awake, her blue eyes darting around alertly. I didn't manage to sleep, but I feel very heavy and drowsy and groggy now. Mum stands up and grabs her bag.

"Come on, Janine!" she says, towering above me. I blink blearily and stand up. I grab my things and help Mum, who is struggling to lumber out our two giant suitcases. People have already started to push their way towards the door, filing past, waiting to get out of the train, so the path is already crowded, but Mum is determined. She gives one of the suitcases a big push, and it shifts to the path. People groan. They can't get past now. I go red and try to push the suitcase to help Mum, but it won't budge. Eventually, after much struggle and humiliation, we get both suitcases out onto the platform. The people behind us are angry as they walk past us. Mum curses at them.

"Mum..." I tut.

"They could've helped me, and none of this would've happened," she snaps.

We stagger out of the train station, dragging our suitcases with us. Mum ruffles in her handbag for her map, almost tipping everything out of it. I yawn. She glances at me and takes a deep breath.

"Don't worry. I know it's late; I found a bed-and-breakfast, and I've phoned and booked us a night there." She winks, and I smile.

"Is it far?"

"It should only be around ten minutes from here," Mum says, picking up her suitcase again. She turns back to her handbag, finally finds her dog-eared map and straightens it out carefully. I look up at the sky. The sunlight glows soft and golden like honey, but I know it must be later than seven by now.

We stop and get fish and chips from the quiet pub downstairs as soon as we arrive. Then, both exhausted, we trudge upstairs to our room. I kick off my shoes and collapse onto the bed. Glancing at Mum's watch, I see that it's just a few minutes past eight, but I'm ready to sleep. Then I notice: there's only one bed.

"Are we sleeping in the same bed?" I ask Mum. She nods wearily before stepping into the bathroom. I don't take it any further. I just move to one side, hug the crisp sheet to my face and fall asleep there and then, without even taking off my jeans.

I hear Mum come back into the room a few minutes later, but my eyes are glued shut and I instantly melt away.

3

Cameron

I wake up at around seven. Pa's gone to check on crops and Ma's already outside too, running various errands. She made me porridge. It's already cold and stiff in the bowl. I wolf it down anyway. Paul would've made a fuss and Ma would've made him a fresh bowl, but I munch on it quietly.

I stumble outside, blinking blearily in the bright daylight. Ma nearly knocks me down by the door, she's in such a rush.

"Cam! C'mon, help me with this." She says, red-faced and huffy. She's holding glass bottles, almost overflowing with fresh milk, though her expression is sour. She's worried about Paul. She always is. It's because he acts like a total idiot in the city with his friends, and does stupid things that get him into trouble. Lately he's started drinking a lot, which angers Pa to no end. He frowns every time anyone brings up Paul and shakes his head disapprovingly. It's always easy to spot Ma's reaction when she's thinking about him, too. Her cheeks set on fire and her mouth tightens in a woeful, wobbly line and she looks like she's about to sob for her poor little Paulie.

"Cam!" she says again. I grab the bottles and follow her as she totters out of the cottage door, through the stone path, down the muddy hill and into the marketplace. Other people have already set up their stalls too. Ma chats with them as we get to our stall. She keeps chatting cheerily, her mood uplifted by this, Paul forgotten for the moment.

4

Janine

"Come on, Janine..." I hear Mum grumble. Slowly, I sit up and open my eyes. I close them back immediately. There's the bright glare of the sun in my eyes and all I want to do is go back to *sleep*. I let out a drowsy groan, muffled by the pillow.

"*Janine.*" I slowly turn over and look up at her, forcing my eyes open. Mum tosses me a bundle of clothes I'd packed specially for this morning – my best jeans and the expensive white top I got for my birthday a few months ago. While I'm in my knickers though, there's a rap at the door.

Mum looks as horrified as I am. "Er, who is it?" she asks delicately.

"Room service." A voice barks back at her.

"No – no, thank you!" Mum says politely. I hear the room service person mutter something under their breath about their job and how awful it is, but they're gone. I grin at Mum. She laughs, and then goes back to frowning over the dog-eared map in her hand. I quickly slide into my clothes and push my enormous suitcase towards the door.

"Ready?" Mum says, looking up. She smiles brightly. "Let's go, darling!"

We rush down the narrow, winding set of stairs into a breakfast room. People are already finishing up, but Mum takes my hand and we both select plates and food. When we're sat down, I eat my breakfast quickly, while Mum delicately nibbles on her slice of toast. She only starts eating quicker when she sees that people are already returning their room keys. We hurriedly run back upstairs to get our things and leave. Getting all our stuff downstairs is quite hard. The stairs are rather shabby and dangerous-looking, but the only thing we can do is begin lumbering those monstrous suitcases downstairs. Mum and I pile our baggage and shakily pull it down after us, before we cross the last stair and we fall down messily at the bottom. The receptionist raises an eyebrow upon noticing us, but Mum sneers at him and he looks away quickly.

"Let's go, Janine," she mutters, dragging her suitcase behind her. I sigh and follow after her.

"Are we lost?" I dare to ask. We're surrounded by greenery: no houses, no shops, just a lonely, dusty road and fields of grass. Mum frowns and doesn't reply. She's clinging onto the map like her life depends on it; her suitcase is dumped on the ground nearby.

"I don't know." Mum finally admits, looking around. There isn't even anyone we can ask for directions – the place is deserted. We're practically in the middle of nowhere.

"Moo!" there's a sound from behind us. My heart does a somersault and I break out in cold sweat.

"What was that?!" I exclaim, gripping Mum's arm. She looks slightly startled by the sound too. We look behind us: there's a boy with a cow, both gazing curiously at us.

"Are you alright?" he asks. I stare at him; he has blond hair, lighter in colour than any I've ever seen in my life. His eyes are soft and blue. He looks the same age as me, maybe even younger, but he's so calm and sensible that I feel a little comforted and I give a small smile.

"Yes," I say, and it's true, but I glance anxiously at the cow. "I... We're from the city. I've... never seen a cow up close before. Sorry." His cheeks dimple as he smiles back. I can't tell if he's being friendly or if he finds this funny.

"Are you from around here?" Mum suddenly chips in. He nods, patting the cow with one hand. "Right," Mum says, inhaling sharply, looking like she's beginning to trust him. She then walks up to him with her map and proceeds to explain where we need to get to by pointing at different spots. She's cautious about it, crouching down a little so that he can see the map too but being careful not to get too close to the cow.

The boy seems confused at first, but a minute later seems to understand and gently pushes the hand that Mum's holding the map with to one side.

"I live just outside this village, on a farm," he says, gesturing towards a chalky yellow road. He slowly gives Mum some directions that she seems to comprehend, then disappears with his cow after giving me another shy smile. By the time I look away, Mum has already started trekking down the path with the heavy suitcase towing behind her. I haul my own suitcase off the ground and run after her to catch up.

It's eleven in the morning. We're standing outside our new home. I gape at it. It is *massive*.

So is the village, actually. I mean, not compared to the city, but it's not the miniscule hole in the middle of nowhere that I expected it to be, I suppose. As we walked through it earlier, I saw plenty of shops, loads of other little cottages and houses pottering the streets, and lots of people. I noticed a couple of children too. We're not as isolated as I thought we'd be.

But now, we're outside the mansion. I grin to myself in glee; *our* mansion. Mum even puts down the map to have a proper look at our house herself.

"Well?" she says, beaming. I run up and hug her. Then Mum starts talking.

"Oh! We have to see the *blah, blah, blah* about the house... since I inherited it, I have to prove *blah, blah, blah*, and sign a few *blah*s, *blah*. *Blah*? Janine!" My head snaps into focus again.

"Yes," I say. "You have to see the... person. You have to sign the, erm, you know." Mum shakes her head disapprovingly.

"Thanks for paying attention," she says.

So for the next hour, we hang around at some man's office, who makes Mum sign about a hundred sheets of paper and talks on and *on* about things I don't even bother to try to understand. I sit there, fidgeting the entire time, looking hopefully at Mum each time she looks like she's about to stand up to leave. Each time she doesn't actually stand up, I sink down a bit lower in my chair disappointedly. In fact, by the time, she really does stand up, I realise a few seconds too late because my eyes are level with the desk.

"So, what's going on? Can we move in, just like that now?" I ask Mum when we're outside, back onto the street. She gives me a big grin and nods.

Mum takes out the large, metal key the man had given her at his office. It's rusted and looks kind of ancient, but she's staring at it like it's the most precious thing in the world. She ever-so-gently slides it into the lock, and a few clicks later, the large oak door swings open. An enormous hallway greets us, dotted with various paintings. A few are landscapes – I grimace and express my disgust aloud upon seeing one of a naked lady.

Mum's looking at them too, with great interest. "These aren't in fashion at all," she says curiously, placing one finger upon the painting of the naked lady.

"They seem pretty old," I remark, looking away. Mum nods eagerly.

"Yes! They must be worth a lot..."

Leaving our suitcases in the hallway, I skip into the first room, Mum close after me. I push open a door that takes so much effort, it makes me wonder: when was the last time someone was in here? As soon as I'm inside, I blink rapidly for a few seconds. The curtains are drawn down low, so there's barely any light in here. I walk across the room inquisitively; my shoes make a satisfying *clunk* each time they hit the wooden floor. I grab hold of one of the heavy mauve curtains and yank it to one side. Immediately, the room is illuminated.

"Wow." Mum says, walking in herself. It's a lot bigger than I realised. I suddenly see something strange.

"Mum," I say. "Why are those sheets covering the furniture?"

"Hmm?" she says distractedly. She's looking out the window, which gives a brilliant view of what must be the garden.

"Those sheets," I repeat. "Those white sheets."

She starts to walk back towards me. "To stop the things from gathering dust, I think." she says.

"Can we take them off?" I say after a pause. Mum shrugs. She places a hand on what I think must be an armchair, but is covered so I can't really tell. Then, without warning, she tears off the sheet. I was right. It's a beautiful, oak armchair with a soft, plush, red seat. I leap onto it and almost bounce right off. Mum laughs.

"What next?" she asks, eager and hungry-eyed.

And so, we uncover every piece of furniture in the house, racing from bedroom to bedroom and just yanking off the sheets like lunatics. By the time we realise that we really shouldn't have, that those dust sheets were there for the sole reason of protecting that beautiful antique furniture, it's already the afternoon, and we've explored the whole house, chosen our rooms and made ourselves at home. My clothes now sit in the great wooden wardrobe in my bedroom, which is on the top floor. Mum's bedroom a few doors away – I wouldn't feel comfortable with her too far away. I think it must be one of the smallest rooms in the house, but it's got massive mullioned windows that have a brilliant view of the street outside.

Mum's bedroom is quite lovely too. It's big and beautiful, with one of the largest and most princessy-looking beds I've ever seen plonked down in the middle. There are loads of guest bedrooms. They're all almost identical: six picture-perfect rooms with fitted golden doorknobs, medium-sized beds next to large rustic windows. Some of these windows overlook the garden, which Mum thinks is absolutely glorious. I don't really share her opinion – it's ridiculously overgrown, with grass reaching up to your knees and weeds littering the place. You can hardly even see where the flower beds originally were. But there is a big, beautiful cherry tree in the corner, with a rusty wind chime hanging over one branch, the yellowing metal rods lolling below. I absolutely love it to bits. Mum told me that we can eat the cherries growing on the tree; they're quite ripe, she tells me, and they'll go bad if we wait much longer. Well, I don't know about eating them, I can't say I trust the tree enough (it must be absolutely filthy, I'll stick to shop-bought, thank you very much) but she also said that every year, before the fruits form, little pink flowers bloom all over the tree, and I can't wait for that next spring.

Mum's in the kitchen right now. It's been modernised, unlike the rest of the house, and she's tidying everything up. She's really happy to be here. She's in love with this place already.

And me? Despite how I felt when she first mentioned the idea of moving to me, I think I may be in love with it too.

⁕⊰⟨⟩⊱⁕

5

Cameron

It's Sunday morning. Only Ma and I are at church (like most Sundays) because Pa is far too busy working on the farm, and Paul, of course, is far too busy being a general nuisance with his friends up in the city.

I look around the hall, but that girl's ma isn't here. I can't help but feel a bit disappointed. Still, today's Sunday, so I don't have to help Pa out with work. I have the whole day to myself. So as soon as the sermon is over, I walk back to our cottage with Ma, get changed hurriedly out of my stiff Sunday clothes and head out.

It's a great day outside – really warm and sunny… not a cloud in the sky. At the market, all stallholders are busy making decorations for the summer festival, which is in just over two weeks. Every year, the whole village holds a festival; it's really cool, I get to stay up till really late because it's like one massive party. I'm not kidding. There's music: Pa actually stops working for once and dances with Ma. Even Paul decides that it's good enough for him, and turns up, flirting with pretty much every woman in sight because of how blindingly drunk he gets. It's an absolute blast.

Maybe that new girl will turn up there.

6

Janine

It's been an entire week since we've moved here, to the Cotswolds. It's going so much better than I ever dreamed it would. First of all, we have our beautiful house. Secondly, Mum's found a job. She looked around the market a few days ago and saw an advertisement at a stall selling clothes that are imported from Belgium. She'll really be in her element there. Mum loves clothes.

She hasn't started work yet; the owner of the stall told her that there was no point in starting just before the summer festival, which is in about three weeks, I think. Everyone we've encountered so far has insisted it's amazing. Apparently, the whole village holds some sort of party. I suppose I'm quite excited for that.

Mum and I have come face to face with the first problem of owning a house as big as ours: it's too big. I know, I thought I'd never say that after having lived in our tiny flat, but it's a lot more work than Mum and I expected. When you think about living in the countryside, you think it'd be calm and relaxing, but this aspect of it is not. I hate cleaning. Though Mum kept a rosy smile on her face and hummed quietly to herself as she worked, I preferred to keep a cross silence.

I've been to the market once before, and Mum's taking me again now. I look around curiously.

"Lots of stalls, aren't there?" Mum says, smiling. I can see what she means – there are dozens of them, lined up next to each other like soldiers.

"Fresh vegetables! Three bowls for one pound!" one woman shrieks from behind a cashier desk. At the same time, an old man bellows from the other side:

"Good, ripe veggies! Get your veggies here! Three bowls, one pound, three bowls, one pound!" I glance at the woman. I expect her to be furious, but she just looks slightly ruffled and more competitive than ever, and barely even pays attention to him. I briefly wonder for how long they've been rivalling today.

"What are we buying?" I ask Mum.

"I was thinking of getting some fruit," she says thoughtfully. "You know, get healthy and such." She nods importantly, although a few minutes later, I see her eyes drool at the sight of some pastries that one woman is selling. They're fresh out of the oven, and the warm, sugary smell drifts for miles.

In the end, we circle back to them after visiting most of the other stalls in the market and buy a small paper bag of them. We finish them all on the way back home.

Mum cooks some baked beans, with sausages that we bought from the market. We eat at the kitchen table, like we've grown used to doing, and then each take up a job: I wash the dishes and Mum sweeps up the floor. Like every evening, Mum tries to peek over my shoulder to make sure I'm doing the job properly, and like every evening, I pretend not to notice, even though it makes me cross. I huff to myself. Not expecting this, Mum starts from behind me and hurriedly finishes sweeping up.

One thing I never realised would come with the package of living in the countryside is the sheer silence of it. It makes sense, because this village isn't big or densely populated, and there isn't another one around here for miles and miles... but now, as I lie in my bed, I listen. I just listen. It sounds absurd, but I just listen to the silence. The magic of it is that the only sounds there are belong to nature: owls hooting, and dogs barking distantly. In the city, I sometimes couldn't sleep for the sounds of the cars, zooming past, or – much worse – roadworks, drilling away. But in here in the Cotswolds, the wind chime in our garden is about the loudest thing I can hear, and, caught up in its lulling, irregular melody, I fall soundly asleep.

When I wake up, it's because Mum's shaking me. I nearly cry out.

"Mum! What's wrong?" Then I look at her closer, and see that she's smiling. "What is it?" I say again, but calmer.

"Come into the garden," she says, pulling my arm.

Slightly confused, I stumble out of bed and follow Mum down two flights of stairs, then finally into our garden.

"What?" I ask. I look down at my feet, and realise that I'm barefoot on the grass. The morning dew tickles my toes.

Mum beckons towards the cherry tree. "They're amazing," she says impatiently. She's holding a bright, wine-red cherry in-between her finger and thumb. She's not holding it too tightly, but a few blood-red drops squeeze out of it; Mum hardly notices. "Have one!" she insists. I swallow hard; it looks a bit too ripe.

"What?" I say, grimacing slightly.

"It's just a cherry, Janine, darling!" Mum says, fingering it with a fascinated look on her face.

"Hmm," I mumble. Mum smiles.

"Fine... Now, how about some breakfast?"

I chew on my porridge noisily. We forgot to buy cereals yesterday. I've never really liked porridge.

"Did you add sugar?" I slur through my mouthful.

"Yes," Mum says; she frowns, but it fades quickly and she maintains her calmness. "So, how did you sleep?" she attempts.

"OK." Her eyes are on me, but I don't add anything.

"Me too," She replies cheerily.

"Do I have to finish this?" I ask. The amount of porridge in my bowl just seems to multiply the more I attempt to finish it.

"Throw it away if you like," Mum says, staring grimly at her own untouched bowl now too. I nod and walk over to the bin. The porridge clumps together in a grotesque way, and falls in a slimy heap.

"Are we going out today?" I ask, trying hard not to feel hungry now. Mum shrugs.

"Do you want to? I don't really feel like it," I look outside through the kitchen window. It was sunny earlier this morning, but now it's slightly grey and looks like it might rain. Mum's face suddenly lights up.

"Oh!"

"Yes, Mum?"

"I've just remembered. I saw our neighbours the other day. A small family; just one child. From what I can make out, they're very, very rich – or used to be, anyway."

"Hmm," I say.

"Their child is really clever, you know; supposed to be one of the best kids in the school. I found out at the market, at the stall I'll be working at. Good heavens, not from them. They're not very friendly. Frankly, I think they rather turned their noses up at me. Humph." She continues crossly.

"Well then, we won't want very much to do with them." I declare, and Mum smiles.

I get up and absent-mindedly trail around the house. I stop in the front room and perch on the armrest of the big sofa. From there, I look out the window – not really seeing through it, just staring into space. I hear Mum clutter around with the dishes from the kitchen.

Suddenly, something catches my eye from outside. I sit up slightly straighter and try to see out the window. I'm so startled by what I see that I feel the blood rush from my head to the tips of my fingers. I don't move an inch.

Just outside our house is a girl; a tall, wide-eyed, Black girl staring right back through the window at me.

7

Winnie

I gawp at the girl in the house. I want to stop, I can tell that it's unnerving her, but I can't help it. A gust of wind suddenly blows, and I shiver and rub my bare arms, breaking my gaze for the first time in about two minutes. When I look back, she's gone.

I sigh and spin round on my heels to head back to my house. I don't think I'm allowed to be out, because my mother was cleaning the house and I should've been helping her, but I managed to slip away before she could protest. Suddenly, I hear running footsteps behind me.

"Wait!" a voice shrieks. I look behind me, and to my surprise, the small girl is running up to me. Well, not that small, actually; now that she's next to me, she looks a lot taller.

Without meaning to, I survey her silently and raise an eyebrow: she is an absolute mess. Her hair is sticking up like a bird's nest, and her clothes fall raggedly about her body. She looks like a scarecrow. On top of that, she's glaring at me, scowling irritably.

"Yes?" I ask coolly.

Her expression darkens. "What do you mean?" Her ears go red, and her brows are furrowed. I'm normally quite bold, but I don't really know *what* to say to her now. Does she want me to *apologise*? Never.

"You were staring at me through my window," she says, walking closer to me. She looks like an angry little man, squaring up to me. I scoff.

"...I wanted to be friends." I say. I shock myself with it too. What was *that*? I never tell the truth so bluntly.

Her face changes, and I can't quite decipher it now. She looks surprised, more than anything, I think. "What?" I throw at her.

"Nothing." she retorts feistily. I don't reply for a second. Then,

"You weren't expecting it?"

She shrugs. That means no.

"OK." she says.

"OK, what?" I demand.

"Let's be friends."

I'm slightly thrown aback at this.

"Fine," I hesitate for a second. "I'm Winifred." I look at her sharply, expecting to see her in stitches. She doesn't react though.

"I'm Janine." When I don't comment upon this, she adds, "I know. I've got an old granny name too." I can't help but smile at her.

"Can I call you Winnie?" she asks.

"Of course." I tell her. Then, when neither of us says anything for a few moments, I stutter,

"I, I live next door," she follows my gaze to my house, on our left.

"Cool. I... well, you know where I live, don't you Winnie?" she replies, smiling mischievously with her eyes. Before I can refrain from it, my mouth stretches into a smile, too.

We're both silent and awkward again when our grins droop away a few seconds later. I start really looking at her: at the way she stands with her feet a little bit apart, how her fists are clenched tightly. Janine looks so feisty. Like... she looks like she's ready to defend herself at any given time. She sits down on the grass.

"You're going to get dirty," I tell her before I can stop myself.

She looks up at me – I now loom over her – and smirks.

"And?"

"Won't your parents be angry?"

"I live with my mum. She doesn't really care."

I widen my eyes. "You're lying,"

She actually laughs. "I'm not. And even if I was–"

"*Were*," I correct her sharply. "Even if you *were*."

"Right," she says, a touch irritated. "Even if I *were*, it's a bit late for that," she turns to show me the wet, green mark all over the back of her jeans. I roll my eyes.

"Winnie; I told you, it's fine, I won't get told off," she says to me.

"You're sure?"

She smiles at me. "Yes." Unexpectedly, she stands up and her thin, pale hand grabs mine. I glance at her.

"We're friends," I say. I don't know if it's a statement or a question, but she seems to take it in her stride, nodding and squeezing my hand lightly. Mine starts to sweat, and I get embarrassed by that, but at the same time, I'm too embarrassed to pull away too.

"We're friends." She parrots back.

"Winifred!"

There's Father's voice. I turn and there he is, at the window, eyeing me beadily. He's clearly just gotten out of bed. He works at the train station, and has been working night shifts lately, so on his free days he sleeps.

"What are you doing out there?" he croaks drowsily, rubbing his eyes.

I open my mouth to reply, but then Mother's voice interrupts swiftly from inside.

"Oh, leave her, she's just enjoying the sunshine."

I swallow hard, embarrassed that Janine is watching all this.

"Winifred, come inside, you need to help with the cleaning!" Father demands, frustrated that Mother is trying to get me out of this.

"Mother, please can't I stay out just a little bit longer?" I plead.

"Play for as long as you want!" she tells me.

Thinking I've gotten out of this, I allow myself a small smile and turn back to Janine, about to apologise for that. Before I can, Mother cuts through again, her voice sounding smaller:

"Although..." I notice that Father's gone now. "...you know those rugs are a nightmare. Please, Winnie."

It wouldn't be fair at all to let her do it all on her own, and she'll be upset with me if I don't help. There's nothing for it.

"I have to go, Janine." I say hurriedly.

8

Bea

I take a cloth to the bathroom and run it under cold water in the sink. It weighs down in my hand. I hear Gran trying to push her coughs down, and I hear the wheezing eruption that follows and I swallow hard. I wring the cloth and watch as the clear, icy water trickles back down the drain. Gran continues to cough in her room. I stumble towards her. She's on the bed, sitting up on her elbows, shaking. Her eyes are watery. The cough fades out, but when she breaths in, it still sounds raspy. I take the damp cloth and lay it over her forehead as she sinks back down, exhausted. I watch her and my chest feels like it's about to explode. I feel helpless. What am I supposed to do? I teeter anxiously around her, fussing over her blanket and her pillows and finally sitting down at her bedside and placing my now feverishly hot hand over Gran's frozen, leathery one. I take my other one and slide it underneath her palm so that now her hand is sandwiched between both of mine. My heart surges with hope. Gran's eyes flutter for a moment before she sinks to sleep.

9

Janine

The next morning, I'm brighter than usual. I actually have a friend!

After breakfast, I bound outside into the front yard. The sun feels like a warm blanket on my back, and the slightly overgrown grass tickles my bare feet through the slippers I'm wearing. I look around. Winnie's not here. I can't help but feel disappointed, even though we didn't arrange anything.

"Boo!" I jump. Yes! She's here, behind me now!

"Winnie!" I exclaim. "Are you alright?"

She smiles in a sort of sly way. "Yes. Sorry about that. I had to help my mother before I could come out."

I grin back at her. "So… they still let you come out today?"

"They almost didn't, but I convinced them." she says. "…If it were up to Father, I'd be studying all day, cooped up in my room."

I glance nervously at Winnie's house behind us, wondering if her parents will come to take her inside again. Shrugging this off, I ask,

"So… what do you want to do?"

"Well," Winnie starts. "You're new here, so maybe I could give you a bit of a tour,"

"Great!" I beam, and rush off to tell Mum that we're going out.

First, Winnie shows me the sweet shop. I hadn't noticed it before, because it's sort of hidden around the corner of an alleyway. When I try to go in, however, Winnie stops me.

"I accidentally dropped a jar of chocolate limes about two weeks ago, and it smashed," she explains apologetically. "The shop owner made it very clear that he doesn't want me to show my face here again. If he does, he'll tell Father... and he probably won't be very happy." I nod understandingly, but my mouth secretly waters at the sight of the sherbets in the window. Winnie drags me away to our next stop.

"Have you seen the market?" she asks me. I start to nod, but she cuts me off.

"No, not the stalls... I mean, have you seen the *other* market?"

I frown. "What other market?" She starts to smile in her sly way.

"Come with me," she takes me by the hand and starts to run; it takes all I can manage not to fall over. She leads me past the stalls, in the centre of the village, to a more secluded spot that stinks so badly, I think I might throw up.

"Oh, I forgot. It's Monday, it's not on today," Winnie says. She looks disappointed.

"What's usually here?" I ask her hopefully, pinching my nose.

"It's an animal market," she explains. "People come here to sell pigs, sheep; ponies too, sometimes, if we're lucky. The local farmer comes down here too, to sell some of his piglets from time to time... and sometimes, in the late summer, to buy some more animals for his farm."

"Oh," I say. "Well, that explains the smell." I remark matter-of-factly. She laughs and we run out of the empty animal market together.

"Oh!" she says, as if she's had an idea. "Speaking of the local farmer – would you like to go down to his farm and see him?"

I'm a bit wary. "You haven't done anything to upset *him*, have you?" Winnie smiles, but looks slightly offended.

"No, of course not."

I laugh silently at her and follow her down the path she's already racing down.

"Is it much further?" I complain.

"Oh, come on, Janine," Winnie says, irritated, tugging at my hand. "Only to the top of this hill and we're there!" I huff, but will my bony legs to go faster.

"There!" she exclaims. "Was that so hard?"

We're at the top. I look around and, in the midst of empty green fields, there is a cosy farmhouse with a worn roof, dark, dusty wooden windowpanes and overgrown dandelions reaching up the stone walls. It looks like it's grown right out of the ground.

She knocks at the door. Briskly, a flushed, hot-cheeked woman opens it. She grins at Winnie briefly, her teeth small and neat and square, before turning back to the laundry basket she cradles under one arm.

"Oh – hello, girls, can I help? Are you lost?" she says inattentively.

Winnie looks disgruntled but gently corrects her. "...I'm Winnie. I'm in the same class as –"

"Oh, yes, of course, that's right, hello, dear." the woman dismisses her hurriedly. "Are you alright?"

"Oh, I'm ... I just wanted to show my friend here around the village."

"Yes, yes, lovely." The woman nods quickly, frowning at her laundry basket. Her eyes flitter from one spot to another as she counts the things she has to do.

"This is Janine," Winnie says, pulling my arm and getting her attention again.

"Good morning." I say uncomfortably. The woman gives me a rosy smile, brimming with genuine friendliness although she doesn't really know what's going on. Her eyes are warm and homely, like a cup of tea, and it makes me relax a little.

"Alright girls, you're free to stay if you want, but I've got to run off to the market quickly." she says, her words stumbling over one another. She waves and smiles again, waddling back into the house. Before turning round the corner of the hallway, she spins back around and says,

"Oh! I have some nice fresh flapjacks that I baked just this morning, if either of you girls would want one?... Just in the kitchen, Winnie'll show you, go on." And she disappears. Eager Winnie grabs my hand and leads me into the kitchen, where we find the crumbly flapjacks on a plate on the table. She helps herself. I'm too shy to take one immediately, but Winnie hands me one and I bite into the flaky, oat-filled pastry keenly. She seems ready to go into the rest of their house too, but as soon as we're finished, I drag Winnie back outside.

"Thank you, ma'am," I call into the house to the woman. I hear a warm chuckle in reply from inside.

"Let's go, Winnie." I say, starting to walk away. She is silent. I spin around to see her staring curiously into the house. I follow her gaze and see a boy looking back at me. I can't place where I've seen him before, it's so frustrating... but, wait! He was the boy that gave us directions into the village on the day we arrived! I slowly walk closer to him. I rack my brains, thinking of something to say. I kind of *have* to say something, don't I?

"Hi," I say awkwardly.

He starts to laugh nervously. "Hello," No one says anything for a moment, which is strange, because Winnie and I aren't really the quiet type. Wait... Winnie? I look at her. She looks stunned, I can't understand why. In fact, she hasn't stopped looking at the boy since she saw him.

"Winnie?" I say, nudging her. "Winnie!"

But it's no use. It's like she's under some spell.

10

Winnie

In front of me, in the farmhouse, is Cameron. He's looking at me like I'm crazy. I want to stop staring, but I can't quite pull my gaze away.

His eyes are deep and blue, like the sea. His hair looks like threaded gold – it's shiny, the colour of dried wheat... and it flops to one side adorably. I know him from school. He's not very clever, but he is just beautiful. I feel a sudden tug at my arm.

"Winnie." Janine, beside me, whispers. I shrug her off and finally come to my senses, dragging my eyes away from him.

"Shall we go now?" I say brightly. Janine rolls her eyes at me and throws Cameron an apologetic smile.

"Do you know each other?" I exclaim jealously, before I can stop myself. He raises his eyebrows and I instantly regret my outburst, but Janine is already replying.

"We've met once before," she says. Now she's staring at him. I can't hide my outrage, and try desperately to get her to look at me, but they're both smiling at each other now, and it's almost too much to bear.

"What's your name?" he asks Janine, stepping closer, and completely ignoring me.

"Janine... what's –"

"I'm Cameron." The grin on Janine's face is tight enough to split her cheeks in two. Janine gestures to me.

"This is my friend Winnie," she says, seeming almost shy.

"I know Winnie, we're in the same class at school," he says patiently, giving me a weird smile. Janine looks very embarrassed. I feel embarrassed too. It makes me feel quite

35

ashamed to think what Father would say if he saw me right now.

"So," I start, slipping my hand into Janine's as we amble through the market to get back home. "How did you two meet?"

Janine slaps my arm playfully. "He gave me and my mum directions on the day that we first arrived here,"

I nod in acknowledgement. "Do you think he likes me?" I think aloud after a few seconds of silence.

Janine splutters with laughter. "I don't know, Winnie! The way you kept staring at him…"

"Stop! Be honest." I reply, scowling.

"I was." she grins.

"Hmm," I say, annoyed. At last, we're back in the patch of grass in front of our houses. I unlink my fingers from hers.

"Do you want to meet up tomorrow? " She nods at me eagerly, her feet trailing her towards her front door. Then I remember.

"I can't any earlier than three; Mother won't let me out of her sight, but she has an appointment at three, so she won't be able to do anything about it."

"Oh," Janine groans. "Oh, it's four already… I'm sorry, I didn't notice it had gotten so late… do you think your mum will mind?" she asks. I consider this.

"I don't *think* so," I say thoughtfully. I'll probably be in trouble if Father is home, but I think he's already at work again.

I heave open the big wooden door and go inside.

"Mother!" I call up the stairs. Then I notice that there is music playing from our rusty old radio in the hallway. It echoes all around the house.

"Oh, you're back," Mother says, bouncing down the stairs.

"Sorry I'm late."

She gives me a weary smile. "It's fine."

I hesitate. "Is… Father at work?"

She nods. "Come here." She says, pulling me into a hug. "Thank you for helping me today."

"You're welcome."

"Your father exaggerates a lot. You're great, you know that. You should be allowed out if you want to go out."

I smile. "Thank you."

It's amusing to remember Janine with her face aglow about my house. I agree, it looks quite grand, but inside it's a mess. There's nothing really that suggests wealth inside. All the money we pay goes towards keeping this place in a working condition, because it's so old that it's practically falling apart. We're doing our best, but there is plenty of gossip about us flying about.

Mother doesn't have a job. It's been that way for as long as I can remember – at first, I suppose it was because I was young and needed someone to take care of me, but I think even now Mother just feels more comfortable staying at home. Father works at the train station, of course, and does handyman jobs around the village as a hobby, so he's not home for hours at a time. It's lucky, actually, that he is good at that kind of thing, because there's a lot in our house that's needed fixing lately – the most dramatic being a whole chunk of ceiling crumbling away. It's not totally safe now, but Father did his best and we hope it won't come down again.

He's sitting at the dinner table now, eyes fixed on me.

"I appreciate the fact that you helped. You should do that all the time, instead of sneaking off." He tells me.

"Yes," I say. "I will." He laughs at me, and I feel my face go hot – the lies just seem to pour out. And they're not even credible.

11

Bea

Gran's asleep. Her breaths are short and shallow, like little gasps. I'm sitting beside her bed, holding her soup and the last of her medication, waiting for her to wake up. But I can't. She needs the rest. I decide to let her sleep for a bit longer.

I go to my room and pick up a book. I sit down and try to read it, but it's no use. I keep thinking about Gran and worrying. None of the words are going into my head. I put the book down and tiptoe to Gran's room. I crack the door open. She's still asleep. I wish she would get better. I walk slowly to the side of her bed and, being careful not to wake her up, I climb into the bed next to her. Gran stirs but she sighs and continues to sleep. I curl up beside her, holding her closely and breathing in her smell. I wish she would get better.

12

Janine

I approach our house as the sun glows a fiery orange. Winnie's already inside. I hope her dad wasn't terribly fussed that she was home late.

"Hi, Mum." I call, entering the hallway and taking my trainers off. I stroll into our kitchen to find Mum there, pouring over what seems to be a recipe book.

"What have you got there?" I ask, trying not to giggle. I don't think I've ever seen Mum cook anything past a boiled egg. She can manage cooking things from frozen in the oven, but this is completely new and unexpected. She looks up and smiles.

"Where have you been, darling?" she asks with that motherly look. Her eyes sweep up and down.

"With Winnie," I tell her, sitting down on the chair next to hers at the table. "My friend from next door."

"How nice!" she gushes, looking all soppy again. I change the subject.

"Are you going to cook us something?" I ask her. She seems amused.

"I cook every day, Janine. If I didn't, you'd starve, darling."

I laugh aloud at this. "Mum, they're ready meals. You heat them for ten minutes. That's not proper cooking."

Mum fights off a smile. "I'm very offended that you don't appreciate my culinary skills, Janine." She gives a little burst of laughter and goes back to her book. I stand up to look over her shoulder.

"Let me see," I plead. "What set this off?" For a moment, I don't think she'll reply. Or, at least, not honestly. But she changes her mind, obviously, and says,

39

"While you were gone, I went down to the stall I'll be working at. I found out that you can donate food for the summer festival – in fact, there's a competition for the best cake!"

I frown and nudge her playfully. "Mum, how many times do you want me to say this? You don't cook." I say. Then I notice a glint in her eye.

"Oh, I see." I say, nodding. "Go on then, tell me. What's the prize?"

She leaps to life. "This beautiful set of antique teacups. Oh, it's china… they're so gorgeous. And must be worth *so much*, darling!"

"I didn't know you liked teacups so much, Mum." I remark.

"Well I don't, not really, but they must be so expensive!" she replies, still looking somewhat dreamy.

I blink slowly. "So you want to sell them?" I ask, not quite understanding.

She laughs, as if I'd said the most stupid thing in the world. "Of course not!"

"Then why–"

"You wouldn't understand, you're far too young, darling." She says, waving me off and returning to her cooking book in a hurry.

I turn around to retire to my room for the rest of the evening before dinner, but Mum calls out when I'm at the kitchen door.

"Janine, why are you going upstairs?" she says. I spin around to look at her. She's still got her nose in the cookbook; she hasn't even actually looked up at me.

"Why shouldn't I?" I ask her.

She looks at me and laughs. "It's still so sunny, darling! Go out, have some more fun,"

I can't help but feel a bit miserable – Winnie is inside now, there's no hope of her sneaking back out now. Mum sees my expression.

"Oh, dear," she says. "Has your friend already gone inside?" I nod.

"Well..." she starts, looking thoughtful. "I suppose you could still go out by yourself, right?" I consider this for a moment; yes, that's not such a bad idea. I smile at Mum and thank her before heading back outside for a little stroll.

It's about half past four in the afternoon, but Mum is right: the sun is still blaring out brightly. I squint and find that my feet are leading me towards the market. I'm so lost in my happy thoughts of my friend Winnie... and, I realise with glee, Cameron. In fact, I soon see that I've gone past the market, and am now trekking up the hill that leads to the farmhouse. I stop on my tracks and look around. The sun isn't quite so blinding now; it has a sort of warm, golden hue. I sigh.

"Who are you?" a voice behind me snaps. I jump and turn to face them.

It's a young man, walking up the same path on the way to the farm. I don't reply.

"Hello?" he says obnoxiously. I feel a rush of blood cloud inside my cheeks and I start to speak.

"I'm new here. Who are *you*?"

"None of your business!" he cries in a slurred sort of way that makes me think he isn't completely sober. I take a few steps closer to him.

"Are you drunk?" I ask him curiously.

"No," he says, raising a hand, as if to bat me away. I raise my eyebrows.

He grunts and looks away, not interested in me anymore. For some reason, this annoys me distinctly, and I attempt to talk to him again, though I'm not sure why I'm trying to make conversation with this rude, slightly tipsy stranger.

"So, lovely weather, huh?" I say awkwardly. He spins around and frowns at me.

"What do you want, kid?"

I shrug. He stares at me; I can't decipher his expression. Then, without warning, he drops a heavy, sun-browned hand on my shoulder and I immediately start to squirm. He won't leave me alone, though, and his fingers are digging into my skin.

"Ugh!" I yell, trying one last time to get him off. I glare at him. He's snorting like a pig.

"Who even are you?" I ask, scowling. He finally lets go and I fall back, annoyed.

"My name is Paul," he says, still grinning. "I live in that house, up there."

"At the farm? With Cameron?" I ask, puzzled. "...Are... are you his dad?" He snorts again.

"*No*. I'm only just turning nineteen." he declares. "I'm his brother." he adds, almost proudly. I fight the urge to smile.

"Well, I'm Janine." I tell him.

"...Alright," he says. Neither one of us says anything for a few seconds. Then:

"You friends with little Cam?" he asks.

I say, "Yes. He's... OK."

We're both quiet again, until I tell him quite abruptly that I have to go home for dinner. On my way back, I can't help but smile at the thought that I have already made three unlikely friends.

13

Winnie

The next morning at ten, I open my front door to find Janine, already waiting. She smiles.

"It's sort of become a habit, hasn't it?" she says, her eyes watching me curiously when I don't step outside. "You know, meeting up every morning."

I smile back. "Yes, I suppose it has,"

After a few moments of silence, Janine asks me,

"Why aren't you coming outside?"

I sigh miserably. "I only came to remind you – I can't come out until three. Remember? Mother will be at her appointment then."

"Oh." she groans. A frown knits her eyebrows together. "I guess I'll see you at three, then."

I swallow. "Bye," I mumble dolefully.

"Bye!" she echoes, looking back at me before trudging back into her own house. I sigh and make a point of slamming the front door shut.

"Winifred!" Father calls down warningly from upstairs.

"What is it?" I ask innocently. I hear him mutter something back, but I'm not sure if I was meant to reply or not, so I ignore him and start towards the kitchen to scrub the sticky stains off the countertops. Mother is there, already cleaning but looking sort of nauseated.

"Thank you for coming to help," she says, smiling feebly. After about fifteen minutes of absolutely exerting myself, Father walks in and I, grateful for the chance for a break, straighten my back and look at him.

"Good morning," I say, trying to smile at him.

"Good morning." he repeats, his face hard. I swallow.

"I'm almost done," I tell him proudly. I did it for Mother, but for some reason he makes me feel like I ought to have been doing it for him. I gesture to the countertop I'd been working on but unconsciously show him my sore hands too. He doesn't look impressed, and makes no comment before leaving the room. He leaves the door wide open, to my annoyance. I daren't say anything, though, and kick it shut with my toe.

Mother and I are both silent and still for a second.

"I'm going to vacuum upstairs. You finish here please." Mother says. Then I'm left alone in the kitchen.

Mother gingerly shrugs on her coat. Next to her, Father watches me like a hawk. I stare at him back.

"You will not go out, Winifred," Father suddenly says, as if reading my mind. I nod and try to look sincere; I can tell that he is far from convinced, but he can't really do anything about it if he's with Mother at her appointment.

Or perhaps he *can*.

"Your father will be staying home with you, Winifred." Mother tells me wearily. My jaw drops to the floor and I goggle my eyes at her in outrage.

"Wh-" I start, almost too stunned to speak properly. "No!"

Mother ignores me. "I must go to my doctor's appointment now." she declares, opening the front door before throwing one encrypted glance at Father. My eyes shoot daggers back at her. "Be sensible with your father," she adds, and with that, the breeze scoops her up and away, and the door slams shut like a clam. I'm stuck in this awful little shell by myself.

I groan aloud. I told Janine I'd be able to sneak out... I should've realised that Mother and Father wouldn't trust me enough to leave me by myself.

Suddenly, Father turns to me.

"That's right, Winifred, I'll be keeping a close watch on you." I scowl and turn away. Father doesn't move a muscle behind me. I stomp off upstairs, and when I come back down half an hour later, Father is looking out the window.

"There's a girl outside, asking after you," he tells me. "Is she your friend? I think she's moved in next door, hasn't she?"

"Yes, with her mother," I blurt out before I can stop myself. Oh, poor Janine.

"Hmm."

He grabs his wallet from the coffee table and rummages around in it.

"What are you doing?" I ask curiously.

"Looking for money. We've ran out of eggs."

I don't get it.

He pulls out a few loose coins. "Here. Go and buy eggs. Maybe your friend will want to go with you."

"Really?" I ask. He gives a small smile, the corners of his eyes lifting up a little too, so I know it's real. "Thank you, Father."

"Winnie! Oh, I'm so glad–"

I beam at Janine. "I know, my father let me go out to buy eggs and–"

"Oh, how nice of him!" she replies, one of her hands deftly taking mine. We start to walk towards the market, almost skipping with happiness.

Soon, we get to the market, which is still buzzing with activity. Caught up in conversation, we walk past the stall selling eggs, fresh from the farm, and we have to turn back. My head still tilted towards Janine as we chat, I quickly grab a box of eggs, pay the keeper and continue our discussion as we start to head back.

"– The lady with the jewellery stall, that old man with the vegetables and, oh! The sweet shop owner; those are all the people I've met in here so far." Janine is saying, gazing at me with glinting eyes. I smile.

"You know, I really ought to show you some more of the locals," I tell her earnestly, strolling down a dusty path that leads to our little lane of houses.

Janine groans. "But they're all kind of boring. I mean, there are, like, ten stalls with fruits and vegetables."

"Five," I correct her gently.

"Yes, yes," she says absent-mindedly. "My point is, I'm not going to want to meet every tedious old man who..." she trails off, seeing the thoughtful look on my face. "What?"

"Not everyone in this village is so simple, you know," I start. Her eyebrows go up and meet in the middle, her mouth goes taut. She looks concerned.

"I didn't mean to offend you. Obviously your family's more high-status..."

I burst out laughing. "No, I didn't... you've misunderstood. No, I meant that there is one rather interesting little cottage – and it's down the road from our lane."

Janine's expression changes again, this time to mild curiosity.

Seeing that I've intrigued her, I carry on while still walking and cradling the box of eggs. "You see, there is this rumour – and I say rumour, but it seems very plausible – that there is an actual witch in the village." I'm careful to keep my voice to barely above a whisper, just for the pleasure of seeing Janine lean in closer.

"Really?" she breathes, in a sort of fascinated gasp. I nod importantly.

"Yes, they say she lives in that cottage down there," I say, pointing to the ramshackle, derelict brown house now a few meters away. Janine gulps, totally thrilled.

"Well," she says. "How do you know she's a witch?"

I laugh loudly. "The usual signs. She's old – *really* old. She's like an ancient dinosaur,"

Janine giggles at this. I add,

"And everyone knows that witches live for hundreds of years!"

Her eyes now look like they might fall out, they've gone so big. "Wow, really?" I nod again.

"Being old is a *sure* sign of a witch." I declare.

"Of course," Janine agrees, and we start walking towards my house again. A few seconds later, Janine, unable to resist, asks me,

"What else?" I smile at her inquisitiveness.

"She's very ugly, you know," I say. After a moment, I add, "Well, I've only seen her once, I think, she never comes out of her house – probably for fear of people finding out what an awful creature she really is – but I did remark upon her–"

"Oh, yes, that's a *sure* sign of a witch!" Janine interrupts eagerly, like a young toddler wanting to please.

"Yes," I say, slightly deflated that she'd stolen my punch-line but contented with the situation all the same.

"So..." Janine starts, as if expecting more thrills. I stare at her blandly. Then, I suddenly remember something else that's rather interesting.

"The witch doesn't live alone, you know," I explain slyly.

"Oh?"

"She lives with a little girl – and a strange girl, at that. I've seen her around the village a few times, but she's never breathed a word to anyone, and she's always alone. She sort of reminds me of a lost puppy," Janine frowns in concentration and understanding.

"Oh," she says. "Why don't you try to talk to her?"

"Why would I?" I ask, slightly annoyed by this.

"Well, it might be good fun," she replies, her eyes sparkling cheekily. I grin at her.

"Alright," I say, committing to the challenge. "Now?"

Janine nods, trying not to laugh out loud. "Do you want to knock on the witch's door?"

I giggle anxiously, both of us now jogging back a few paces to get to the odd little cottage. "No, you do it,"

"Are you scared, Winnie?" Janine says, seeming shocked and amused.

I raise my eyebrows. "Are you?"

Neither one of us says anything. Then,

"Fine, I'll do it," I say. I can feel the blood rush through my head; I don't quite know if I'm feeling excited or nervous. Janine, loyal as anything, sticks close behind me as we approach the beaten down, wooden front door of the witch's house.

"Wait," I suddenly say. "What if she casts a spell on us for being bad?" Janine bites her lip, which is worrying, because I was hoping she'd tell me I'm being ridiculous. But, unable to find any other reason to still do it, she replies hurriedly,

"Just... do it anyway." I nod and we slowly step closer and closer until I reach out my hand warily, and let my fingertips touch the smooth, worn wood of the door. I swallow hard, trying not to show how frightened I am.

But I do it.

I give three sharp raps at the door. Everything seems to slow down eerily as I do so – the longest two seconds of my life. I can feel Janine's moist breath, steaming on the back on my neck, and I grimace.

KNOCK. KNOCK. KNOCK...

⚜

14

Janine

I give a loud gulp as Winnie knocks on the door. She tries to hide it, but she looks so ludicrously afraid – not at all like the friend that I know.

The second she's knocked, I bolt away from the witch's cottage, Winnie a millisecond behind me. I laugh loudly, too loudly, it seems, after the silence from what is about ten moments ago, but feels like it took hours.

"Wow!" I laugh. Winnie punches me in the arm playfully and whoops.

"You see? I did your dare," she shouts.

"You did," I admit. "For a second, I didn't think you would."

She scoffs. "What, me? I'd never forfeit a challenge. Ever." she smirks.

"You were terrified, though!" I exclaim, peering at the cottage cautiously. I catch sight of Winnie's enraged expression and almost laugh out loud.

"No, I was not!" she yells, waving her arms about. She forgets the box of eggs and they go flying across the street, landing with a distinctive *smack!* on the pavement a few metres away. Winnie gives a shrill scream that gives me goose bumps along my arm.

"Oh, no," I mutter, approaching the ruined cardboard box. As I get closer, I see that yellow goo is slowly oozing through the small gaps. I glance back at Winnie, who hasn't moved from the spot. Her eyes are closed.

I think of her dad and my palms start sweating.

"I'll get some cash from my mum, Winnie," I call nervously. "We can buy some more eggs. Your parents don't have to find out, you know–"

Winnie suddenly gasps at a movement I don't detect, and spins around. Then I see: a few paces away, standing in front of the gate of their house is the tall man, her father, who talked to me earlier, staring at Winnie with fiery eyes. Looking back at Winnie, I see beads of sweat rolling down her forehead. I wonder for a second if she'll cry.

"Father," she says hoarsely. He breaks their gaze, glancing towards the ground as if he can't bring himself to look at her.

"We were playing, Father." Winnie whispers. I doubt that her dad heard her, but she's silent now and looking away shamefully. I think about asking Winnie's dad if he'd like me to fetch some cash from Mum to buy another box of eggs, but I hurriedly decide I'd better not.

"I told you to come straight home, Winifred." he says, speaking for the first time.

"Father, I'm sorry," Winnie attempts again. "We... we were just playing..."

"I heard you the first time, Winifred."

Winnie gulps.

"I'm very disappointed, Winifred." her dad says. A fat tear rolls down Winnie's cheek at this, and something breaks inside me. When we lived in the city, I would've made fun of anyone who cried, I realise. Biting my lip nervously, I look back at her dad.

"Inside." he demands. "Now." Winnie quickly scurries after him, snuffling to herself. I stare after her. She doesn't look back at me.

I swallow hard. Before trudging towards my house, I throw a last glance at the sad box of cracked eggs on the floor.

When I'm at my front door, I hear a sound from behind me and I jump. It came from the direction of the witch's cottage. In the doorway stands a pale girl, with a look on her that reminds me of a frightened rabbit. Without thinking, I wave and smile at her. She bolts inside her house. I hear the clicking of the lock echo throughout the street.

Silence.

Winnie, of course, doesn't come out for the rest of the day. The next morning, at seven, I bolt down some breakfast cereal with Mum, who has given up on cooking and turned to baking. Her cupcakes that she's just finished are burnt, and they end up in the bin.

"I'll try again in a bit," she says, resting on the sofa. I smile and go outside. Frowning at the sun, I stare at Winnie's door thoughtfully. She might be able to sneak out later, but right now I can hear her mum shouting and decide against knocking at the door. Instead, I walk towards the market to wander around for a bit, but my feet stop before I get to the main road; I'm in front of the witch's cottage. That girl that I saw yesterday – she looked so lonely. Maybe we can make friends.

"Janine!" I hear a voice from the corner that runs onto the main road. Cameron. I grin.

"Hi, Cameron," I say, walking towards him.

"What... what you doing?"

I gesture towards the house. "I just... I kind of want to–"

Cameron's eyes are wide. "A witch lives there, you know. Don't go anywhere near that house!"

Slightly startled, I say, "There's... there's a girl living there. With the witch. I wanted to meet her."

"*Why?!*"

"Well, she looked sort of lonely," I retort stubbornly. Cameron laughs.

"What are you doing here, anyway?" I ask him, changing the subject.

He shows me the two litre bottles he's holding; one in each hand. "Selling milk down at the market," he tells me.

"Need any help?" He shakes his head hurriedly and scoffs, but his knuckles are white and strained.

After a few moments of surprisingly comfortable silence during which we simply stare at each other, I declare,

"Well, I'm going to try to make friends with the girl." Cameron doesn't try to argue, but looks thoughtfully at the cottage.

"Can I come?" he asks after a little bit.

"Yes!" I exclaim gleefully. "Yes."

"Aren't you scared?" he asks me curiously, placing down his bottles of milk. I shake my head proudly, although I'm fearful of the witch herself.

"She's just a girl, Cameron," I say. "Maybe she needs help."

"Yeah," he says after some consideration. "Maybe she needs us to save her or something."

We approach the front door cautiously. Somehow, it's not so exhilarating as when Winnie and me did the knock-door-run prank.

Cameron knocks for me, which is sweet of him, I suppose. Then we wait.

"Do you think she's even in?" Cameron whispers. I shrug and we keep waiting. Suddenly, we hear a movement from inside.

"I think she is," I say, delighted. "But she's probably not going to answer the door." After a few more apprehensive moments, I shout

"We want to make friends with you!"

Cameron falls about laughing.

"Please... please come out!" I continue, through short bursts of giggles. We hear more shuffling sounds from within. Suddenly, the door opens a few inches. I see a sliver of the girl's face.

"Please come out," I repeat, but much quieter. I smile at her and gesture to Cameron next to me.

"We want to make friends," I tell her earnestly, though Cam is frowning uncertainly now.

"Go away." she says shakily. She starts to push the door shut, but I stick my foot in the crack.

"Please!" I exclaim. "We know that you're probably lonely in there and we just–"

"Shh!" she says suddenly. She slips outside and gently closes the door behind her. "My Gran's asleep."

"Oh, sorry," I say sheepishly. We're all quiet for a second, studying each other. I take in her grubby dress that hangs below her knees like rags, her bare feet, her pale skin. I smile and start to speak again.

"I'm Janine,"

Cam takes my cue. "I'm Cameron,"

We wait expectantly for her to introduce herself. She stares back, eyes wide with fear.

15

Bea

I hesitate before replying. "I'm... Bea," I wring my hands absentmindedly. "She's ill. My Gran. That's why she's sleeping. She needs to rest."

"Is she a witch?" the boy blurts out.

The girl nudges him in the ribs. "Cameron!" she hisses. My eyes widen.

"Sorry, Bea, I..." Cameron says, faltering, realising.

"Why would my gran be a witch?" I ask. I'm not angry at all, just taken aback and curious.

"It's just... there's a rumour in the village," Janine explains apologetically.

"That..." I start.

I notice Cameron bracing himself.

I gulp and stammer, "That... would make sense," Janine goggles her eyes at me, not understanding.

"Huh?!" she exclaims. I nod at her slowly and look towards the ground, processing everything. A long lock of my hair falls towards my face. I brush it away distractedly.

"Well," Janine starts, taking a breath, weighing everything up. "Is she old?" she asks.

"Very old. I don't know *exactly*, but it's got to be more than eighty," I answer giddily.

"A sure sign of a witch," she murmurs. What does she mean?

"Why don't you – yourself and the witch... I mean, your gran – get out much?" Cameron asks.

"She has terrible arthritis," I explain, my head still swirling. Cameron and Janine give me blank expressions. "It means that her joints hurt a lot when she moves around,"

"A likely story," Cameron snorts. Janine elbows him sharply. He protests, "What? ... Sorry," He sounded so confident at first. Janine rolls my eyes at him and gesture to me to carry on.

"So she stays in bed, in her room, all day long. She's awfully frail, and quite ill. Her immunity system... could be better. We can't afford medicine, though. She gets some pension money, but not nearly enough, I think. I sell some of her old knitting at the market – her arthritis in her hands and wrists is too bad for her to knit anymore – but it barely gets us any money," I say sadly, in a confusing and long-winded ramble.

"Hang on," she stops me. "If she stays in bed all day, how do you survive? What do you guys eat, and–" I chuckle. I can't help myself.

"I cook for us, obviously, Janine,"

She frowns and nods. Next to her, Cameron looks shocked.

"There's nothing else to tell. We don't have any money for medicine."

I feel a lump forming in my throat. Poor Gran. Then there's a sudden stumbling sound from upstairs. I jump.

"I have to go. Gran has woken up, she can't know I was out without her permission," I mumble miserably, slipping back inside the cottage.

16

Janine

Cameron and I stare after her. I wave half-heartedly, and then, just as abruptly as she'd come, Bea is gone. I'm left with a sense of guilt while I mull over her story. Mum and I have inherited money, quite a lot of it. I wish I could help Bea and her grandma out, but I really don't know how Mum would feel about giving money to what is believed to be a witch. I look to Cameron hopefully. No. His family already has enough mouths to feed without having to help out a poor old woman and her granddaughter.

"Well, that milk won't carry itself off to the market stall." Cameron says.

I laugh. "I thought you were strong enough to carry it off by yourself?"

He smiles and heaves one of the heavy bottles into my hands. We lumber them off towards his family's farm stall – a separate one from his mum's jewellery stall – whilst talking about this strange girl we'd just met.

"Oi Cam," says a voice from behind us. We turn around: it's his brother Paul. He belches loudly, and I try not to grimace too obviously.

"And hello... you, girl, I forgot your name." he continues vaguely.

"Janine." I say quietly. Cameron looks at me curiously, no doubt wondering how I know his brother. He doesn't say anything though.

"Cam, are you too weak to carry those bottles by yourself, mate?" he taunts. Cameron looks at the ground; not in a submissive way, but as to not start a scene.

"Do you need a girl to help you, Cam?"

"Stop that!" I shout suddenly, the bottle of milk almost slipping out of my hand. Paul laughs.

"Woah, steady there, gal."

I scowl at him.

"You're drunk again," I say.

"No, I'm not," he says nasally, leaning on the wall of a nearby building.

"Yes, you are, Paul, you're *drunk.*"

"Bug off, little girl," he says, looking away. I don't say anything to this, but I'm fuming. I feel Cameron's hand on my arm, pulling me away. We walk some more until we arrive at the market.

"He's always like that when he drinks," Cameron tells me. "He must've been at Pa's whiskey again..."

I try to smile, like this is funny.

We don't speak for the rest of the way. When we've dropped off the milk, I suggest,

"Why don't we help Bea sneak out? We can play at my house if you're not busy."

"Yeah, sure."

We go back to the cottage and knock on the front door, patiently this time. Bea appears in a matter of seconds.

"Wh– hi again. What is it?" she says quietly. She opens the door slowly, to make sure it doesn't creak too loudly.

"Do you want to come to my house to play?" I whisper.

"We'll help you sneak out," Cameron adds.

Bea considers this. "But my gran–"

"She doesn't need to know a thing," I interrupt, shaking my head. After some more thinking and a quick dash upstairs, Bea slips back outside and gently closes her front door.

"Alright, she's fast asleep, and she'll doze for at least an hour or so," she says. I grin and lead the way to my house.

"Holy Jesus, you didn't say you live in a mansion!" Bea cries, staring at my house.

"All the houses down here are like this," I laugh. " Me and Cam's friend, Winnie, lives next door, you know. You'll love her,"

"It's so big though," Bea says, not taking her eyes off of the house.

"I'll say," Cameron remarks, impressed. I feel a sudden urge to hug him.

"I haven't actually explored all of its rooms yet," I say to them. "It'll be good fun to do that."

"Yeah!" Bea says. "Wait... are you sure your ma is alright with us being here?"

"We'll soon find out..." I mutter, pushing open the oak door. "Mum!" I yell.

"Yes, darling?" she says, scampering towards the doorway. "Oh! Hello, who are you?"

"Mum, this is Bea," I say, pointing to her. "And Cameron." I place a hand on his shoulder.

"Oh, hello. Ooh! I've made some gingerbread, would you like to taste some?"

I sigh, smiling. "You've been baking again?"

Mum tuts with mock-annoyance. "Hey, it turned out OK. Come on in."

We all sit down on a chair around the kitchen table. In the centre of it, a hot plate of gingerbread sits, the smell wafting in the air around it.

"Go on, try some," Mum says, watching us curiously. Cameron dives in first; he snatches a piece and shovels it in his mouth, so fast he surely can't actually taste anything.

"Ah," he says when he's finished chewing. He looks like he's just sucked a lemon. "My ma... doesn't usually make it with, um, chilli pepper." he breathes in deeply, trying to get rid of the taste in his mouth.

"It's not chilli, darling, it's the ginger. You know, *ginger-bread*."

I take a bite and discreetly spit it straight back out onto a tissue. "Maybe not quite so *much* ginger, Mum," I suggest delicately.

"I like it just fine," Bea says through a mouthful. Mum looks thrilled.

"Oh, thank you, darling." she says, beaming. She takes a piece herself and bites generously out of it. She can't stop herself from crying out. "Oh!" she exclaims. "Perhaps... perhaps it *is* a bit too much ginger." she goes a bit red and carries the plate to the kitchen countertop. I stand up too and gesture to Cameron and Bea to do so as well; I say to Mum, whose back is turned,

"We're just going upstairs to play now, Mum."

"Yes, darling," she replies, looking at me and smiling.

We bound up the stairs.

We're in my bedroom. Suddenly, I feel a bit embarrassed; there aren't any childish teddy bears or anything, it just seems a bit personal. Cameron looks around curiously while Bea plonks down on my chair.

"Whew!" she exclaims. "That's a lot of stairs." I smile at her sympathetically and wave to Cameron to sit down next to me on the bed. He perches on the end of it cautiously, like he's a bit out of his comfort zone too.

"So..." I start. "What do you want to play?"

"Tag?" Bea suggests. I shake my head.

"Sorry, not inside."

She insists, "No, we can go outs–"

"How about we look around in all these fancy rooms, like Janine said earlier?" Cameron interrupts. I flash him a quick smile.

"Great," I agree, getting up. Cam follows my lead and taps Bea's arm to do the same.

"Let's go then!" she exclaims happily, skipping out the room into the hallway and almost falling down the stairs. I try not to laugh and place a hand on her shoulder to steady her.

"What's in this room?" Cameron asks, edging open a nearby door.

"I don't know, actually," I reply, looking into it curiously. The sheets that Mum and I had carelessly thrown off when we'd first moved in still lie melancholically on the floor. I walk in and cough loudly.

"Phew..." Cameron sighs behind me. "So dusty in here." I nod and cover my mouth with my palm, which is warm and slightly damp.

"Wow, look at this," Bea suddenly says, wondering at a painting of a poppy field. Cameron raises his eyebrows, impressed. I can't help but smile smugly.

"Quite nice, isn't it?" I say, skipping a few paces further. I feel like a tour guide. "Let's move on. Um, how about we see the next room?" Bea skips ahead if me as I open the door, pushing me into the wall. I get that Bea is too happy and bubbly to see anything around her, but it's a little tiring, and it's not very nice of her to push in front of me like that.

"You alright there?" Cameron asks, gesturing to me to go first.

"Yup," I say, feeling calmer. I sigh. "Wait, no, it's fine, you can go first."

"No, no..." he falters, unsure of how to respond.

"No, please, go on..."

"B– no, you," he insists. I swallow hard.

"Cameron, come on, just go first, it's no big deal." I say.

He shakes his head and takes a step back. "No, please, you go first."

I wonder whether I should carry on persisting, but it seems rather pointless. I step through the doorway; however, Cameron was clearly expecting me to tell him to go first again, and on impulse, he pushes forward too. I roll my eyes.

"My goodness," I mutter, and he goes red.

"What's taking you so long?" Bea exclaims, scampering back down the hallway to us. "Come on, I thought we could go outside now. It's getting a bit musky and miserable inside." I say. I gaze out a nearby window. It's quite cloudy, but not too dull, so I nod and run the stairs, the other two right behind me with puppy-like eagerness.

"Oh, good, you're all here," Mum says, smiling, as soon as we're at the bottom of the stairs. We're all panting a bit, our hearts beating like drums in our chests.

"What is it?" I ask. I grimace. "More baking?"

Mum stifles an irritated look in her eyes and tells us, "No, darling, but I think your friend from next door is outside. I thought about asking her in, but she looks rather shy."

I snort. Winnie? Shy? "...I'll have a look." I say, and walk to the window. I throw back the heavy curtain. Sure enough, there she is, glancing around nervously.

"Oh," I remark and go outside to see her.

"Janine!" she exclaims, her face lighting up. It's weird; when she's not around other people, she does look a bit shy, or less bold in any case.

"Come in." I say brightly. I usher her inside. "You know Cameron," I say, tugging on his arm. He looks slightly pained to see Winnie, who now looks like she's melting. "And this is Bea," Winnie struggles to take her eyes off Cameron.

"Winnie!" I complain.

"Who?" she says distantly.

"She lives in that cottage down the road, with the witch." Cameron chips in. Winnie's expression quickly shifts. She looks outraged.

"Ugh! Isn't this a bit dangerous?" she asks, looking at Bea as if she's something horrible and sticky on the back of her shoe.

"Hey, stop, Bea's lovely." I say, trying not to make this into a scene. "And who knows if her grandma really is a witch? For all we know, she's just plain Mrs Anderson."

Winnie doesn't say anything further, but juts her chin out in a discreet act of stubbornness and defiance that absolutely no one can argue with.

Winnie, she's like that. She's a zap of electricity; a surge of unapologetic confidence.

17

Bea

My gran is really old. I don't actually know exactly how old, but I remember being much younger and sitting on her lap while she filed through stiff, yellowed albums of black-and-white photographs. I remember her wrinkled smile as she reflected on her past, and the hoarse voice she'd use to tell me bedtime stories. My gran doesn't really smile anymore. Even her eyes droop all the time now as she weakly lies in bed. I don't mind looking after her, but sometimes it seems hopeless.

A while ago, before Gran was completely bed-ridden and was still able to get out and about, we went together to pick up her medicine one afternoon, and I had an idea. What if we had a nurse to come in every couple of days to help? At first, Gran was reluctant, but even then, she knew that she was getting weaker and weaker. I had no clue at the time that she would become quite so frail. Gran eventually agreed, but no one was available, or willing to come to help Gran out. We even put out an advert in the newspaper, and Gran offered over half of her monthly pension, but we still had no success – until a couple of weeks ago, when I returned from the shop to find Gran speaking on the telephone. It was all arranged, and since then, a social worker has been coming in every week to check in on me and Gran. I wish it would make more of a difference. I saw the pity in Janine's eyes when I told her that we're poor.

Gran woke up today just as I was about to step out of the house to go to play with Janine. I panicked and shushed her and soothed head back onto the pillow. Gran didn't complain or fuss at all, and meekly relaxed back. I asked her how she was feeling, suddenly guilty that my poor gran was finally recovering and I was more focussed on my own things. I asked if she felt hungry, if she wanted me to bring in her lunch, or at least a glass of water. I asked if she wanted me to open her window to let in the fresh summer air. I sat beside her, Janine forgotten, and squeezed her hand and kissed her cheek. When I looked closer, I saw that Gran had already fallen back asleep.

18

Winnie

Father told Mother about the mishap with the eggs as soon as she stepped foot through the door. Normally, Mother would've told me off a bit too – not as badly as Father does, but still enough to remind me that she's my mother. However, she looked too drained of energy to do any of that. She said she needed to lie down, and when she got back up an hour later, I heard Mother and Father arguing about something. It ended in tears that Father then coaxed away. I still don't know what it was about.

Anyway, I sneaked out soon after that. Now, I'm in Janine's house.

"You know Cameron," she's saying, her hand on his arm. I stare at it, as if my gaze can shove it right off him. I see his face – maybe it's just me, but I think he looks a bit uncomfortable. I glance at Janine again, at her hand on his arm; every fibre in body screams, but I quash down the jealousy. My eyes try to grip onto his, but he looks like a lost animal trying to escape the zoo.

"Winnie!" Janine suddenly exclaims, looking irritated. She's pointing to a girl I don't know who's standing next to her.

"Who...?" I start indistinctly. I examine the girl – she's wearing some sort of plain dress; her legs are bare apart from a pair of grubby socks that are under her black plimsolls. Her hair is long and shiny but knotted; overall, she looks pretty shabby.

"Bea lives in that cottage down the road, with the witch." Cameron says. He's fingering his wrist where Janine had touched him seconds before. I peel my eyes away and process this.

"Oh, ugh! Isn't this, um, a bit dangerous?" I say. I realise a heartbeat too late how rude that must've sounded, but I can't help but grimace when I look at the girl.

It may be mean of me, but if this girl lives with a witch, she could very well be severely ill. Or worse yet, she could cast her own spell on us. We could *die*. I'm not particularly keen on taking that risk.

"Hey, *stop*! Bea's *lovely*!" Janine says, her voice a little bit forceful. She emphasises every word, like she's still trying to convince herself too. "And who knows if her grandma really is a witch?" she continues feebly. "For all we know, she's just plain Mrs Anderson." She sounded so hesitant saying that. She can't *possibly* expect me to take her seriously.

I raise my eyebrows. The witch is actually Bea's grandmother? The magic is in their blood. I stare at this Bea. She looks so simple; so stupid. She even smiles at me... a happy, sunny smile that makes me feel quite sorry for her. The more I think about it, the more she makes me cringe. So I don't say anything. I simply nod and stare at the ground.

Less than twenty minutes later, however, I'm back at home, cooped up in my bedroom. Mother is crying again downstairs.

Then there's a horrible retching sound, like someone's grabbed onto Mother's stomach lining and yanked hard, turning her inside out. I instinctively get up, and then dither stupidly at the doorway. I can hear Father now, soothing her, and Mother crying loudly. I would be in the way. Not quite knowing what to do, I drift to my window. It looks out into our garden; if it deserves to be called that. It's much smaller than Janine's, and ugly too, with brown shards of porcelain flower pots scattered everywhere, and terribly over-grown... everything. I don't think anyone has been in there in months.

I can see part of Janine's garden too. Her mother is outside, sitting on a bench in the sun. Janine must still be inside with Cameron and... and Bea. Her mother's head suddenly snaps to one side, seeing something I don't see.

"Hello, have you come to play out here?" she asks, grinning. Then I see all three children running, skipping, stumbling outside.

I stand there for a few minutes, watching them all laugh while I turn emerald-green with jealousy. The only reason I left Janine's house was because I heard Mother and Father and feared they were after me.

There's a wheezing sound as the train leaves; it distracts me momentarily.

"My brother Paul is on that train," I hear Cameron say. Suddenly, I can't take my eyes off him.

"Why?" Janine laughs, trying to balance a daisy chain that Bea had made on her head.

"He's staying in the city for a few days... he'll be there for his birthday. Apparently, he's staying with his friends." he continues, sinking down on the grass.

Bea holds up another chain of daisies to his face. "Do you want one too?" she asks. Janine falls about laughing.

"Oh yes, I like your thinking, Bea." She exclaims, grabbing it and making it settle daintily on top of Cameron's golden hair.

"Very pretty," she jokes as Cameron attempts to brush it off. I can't help but giggle quietly to myself. Then, remembering that I'm sulking, my face turns dark again and I quickly regain my composure. I grab my curtains with clenched fists and pull them together violently. It doesn't drown out all the laughing, but it gives me some peace of mind. Lying on my bed in near-dark, I close my eyes; not to sleep, but to relax. Everything is so quiet now, so peaceful. My bed is so soft. I'm gently rocking on my own little hammock of tranquillity; rocking, swaying, floating. Floating away...

My eyes snap open. I look at the ceiling of my bedroom – had I really fallen asleep? For how long? It can't have been longer than a few minutes. My throat feels dry, and I try to remember why I had been so upset earlier. My head is still swimming with distant, fleeting dreams and slight vertigo. My body is glued to the bed. Then it all comes back to me, like a punch to the stomach. Janine; Cameron; everything in-between.

"Tag!" Janine screams from outside.

I put my pillow over my head and shut everything out.

19

Janine

Another week has passed. It's felt like a second. Every day has been carefree fun – no troubles but the usual tiffs that come between children. Well. Winnie seems to have a *serious* problem with Bea, not that the latter seems to worry about it. Poor Bea is… perhaps too simple to be so attentive as to notice those small, hostile acts that would've gnawed at any other person who was subject of them. But not sweet Bea; she seems oblivious on the most part, which is good because at least it doesn't hurt her.

I know that Winnie isn't really a bully – she's more like a territorial sort of dog. A yappy Yorkshire terrier: all bark, no bite. Well, mostly.

I say a quick goodbye to Mum, who's quietly munching on some cupcakes she'd made earlier that morning and stumble outside in my baggy brown shorts. My legs look awfully skinny and pale – a mottled pink kind of colour – but I try not to care and wave at Cameron, who's already waiting outside.

"What do you want to do today then?" he asks. I look at him. His clothes are perfectly ordinary, but on his head, a large straw had perches like a ruffled crow. I snort.

"What is *that*?"

He stares at his shoes, completely humiliated. With one hand, he shoves it off and it falls to the ground in one swift movement.

"Ma made me wear it," he mumbles, not quite looking me in the eye. "Said the sun's too bright to be out without a hat."

I try not to smile and say, "Oh, right. Sorry." He doesn't reply. I hope he isn't *really* mad at me.

"Let's go and get Bea, and then wait and see if Winnie can come out," I say in an attempt to move the conversation forward. Cameron nods and we walk to the cottage in silence.

I knock gently at the door. I know that Mrs. Anderson (the witch) will be taking her mid-morning nap now, so there's no real danger of being heard, but I'm cautious all the same. I'm still not quite sure if I believe all of the witch mumbo jumbo, but I would much rather be safe than sorry. Besides, if Mrs Anderson catches wind of the fact that Bea is disobeying her by going out without permission, we'll probably never see her again.

Soon enough, Bea peeps through the door and smiles at us. In seconds, she's slipped out and we're heading back to the lane of houses where I live to see if Winnie can come. She's already standing there outside.

"Hello," she says. "Hi Cameron," she adds specially.

He grunts in acknowledgement. Winnie is lightly fazed but quickly turns to me.

"What's going on today?" she asks. They all pause to look at me. Cameron's face is still unsmiling.

I try to think. "Not the market, I suppose," Winnie shakes her head violently and Bea shudders silently.

"No, no," Winnie says.

Yesterday, we were playing a particularly thrilling game of tag that started in front of my house but drifted all the way into the market. Winnie, by far the fastest out of all of us, was running around trying to catch us, and we all squealed about shrieking loud enough to wake old Great-Uncle Casper from the grave. I began to weave in and out of the stalls; and that's when it all went wrong. The space in between the stalls is very narrow – enough for me to run through easily, but not Bea too... she of course followed straight after me and at one point, she bumped into me clumsily. It was completely unpredictable and I fell down. Cameron was quick to help me back up, but we had knocked some things off a nearby vegetable stall. We hurriedly picked them all up, but the stall owner was coming towards us fast... and that's when Winnie jumped up to tag us. She dived straight for Cameron, who staggered onto the stall owner and the entire stall collapsed! We bolted straight out, the angry shouts of the market echoing behind us.

So no, we aren't going there today.

"How about we go to the farm?" I suggest, looking to Cameron hopefully. We've been there once since the first time, and though I rather hated the strange, aggressive chickens, and wrinkled my nose at the pigs, I admit that Dolly the cow quite captivated me. It was almost as though she really remembered me from a few weeks ago when we had only just arrived here… the way she tossed her head and gazed at me with those mild brown eyes. Cameron said it was alright to touch her, she wouldn't hurt me. He patted her so hard that dust came off her coat and glinted in the sun like miniscule diamonds. I knew he would never harm her, but this still seemed to me a little brutal, so I just stroked her gently. At this point, I didn't even mind the strong smell that she emitted – behind that was a mellower, sweeter, dustier scent that reminded me of that special smell that babies sometimes have.

Of course I want to go to the farm. Yes, I am all for helping out, maybe even helping his mum with her work, or even his dad with the animals, but seeing Dolly somehow would make it all more special.

"Sure," Cameron shrugs. I grin at him and look to the others.

"Is that OK with everyone?" I ask. Bea beams back at me sunnily.

"It's great! Maybe your ma will let me help with her jewellery again if she has time? …" she adds. Cameron nods indifferently. Bea is thrilled.

I turn to Winnie. She seems slightly taken aback at the suggestion, but eventually agrees.

"Of course I'll come," she says, her eyes gleaming when she looks at Cameron.

After carefully sneaking past the market, we begin to journey up the hill leading go the farmhouse. It takes several hot, uncomfortable minutes and by the time we're there, we're all completely breathless, even Winnie, who kept trying to walk joined at the hip with Cameron. Now we're outside the house. I reach my hand up to knock, but Cameron places his over it and opens the door. Ha. I almost forgot. It's his house.

"Ma?" he calls into the house. "It's Cam, I'm here with my friends!"

She comes stumbling out of the kitchen, rosy-cheeked with her hair done up in a messy ponytail.

"Oh! Hello, dear," she says, smiling. "And… oh, Janine isn't it? And … Bella and Ginny, I know you, love!"

I stifle a laugh.

"Yes, *Winnie*," Winnie says firmly. She doesn't correct her on Bea's name. Cameron's mum takes no notice anyway.

"I'll just be in the kitchen. I'm baking a big birthday cake for your brother, Cam. He's coming home today from the city."

"Alright," he replies, distinctly uninterested.

"Me and your pa got him something well special," she continues proudly. Cameron looks up.

"What is it?" he asks.

His mum just winks slyly. In that moment, she suddenly reminds me of my own mum, although they're not remotely similar in any other way. "You'll see in a few minutes." She says. "His train must just be arriving, I reckon."

"Come on!" Bea suddenly shouts. We all look through the window and she's outside in the field. Winnie slumps outside after her like a slug. I linger behind and wait for Cameron. He stares at me.

"You can go first," I say, gesturing towards the door.

He hesitates. "No, go on."

"Please, Cam."

He shakes his head keenly. "Come on," he says. For a moment, I just stare at him. Then without even knowing I'm going to do it, I hug him. It's an impulsive move and I regret it immediately because he stands there, frozen. I try to pull away, but I feel a small squeeze back and I relax with relief. I don't know how much longer it is before we stop. I smile at him. He's gone a bit pink. I know the feeling; I'm glad we're proper friends again too.

20

Cameron

I don't know what to say. I don't frankly know if I should say anything. What is happening?

I didn't expect her to hug me. I don't think she was expecting to either.

I swallow hard and feel my face go hot. I hope she can't tell.

"Cam!" Ma suddenly hollers. She bustles out of the kitchen. "Your brother! He's walking up to the front door!" I peek out of the window. Sure enough, there he is. He looks miserable; Ma doesn't seem the slightest bit fazed by this. She yanks open the front doors hard it nearly falls off its hinges and runs out so excitedly, you'd think he's been fighting on the battlefields of south France for a year.

He hears Ma and looks up as she comes towards him. I bet the soldiers in south France heard her too.

"Paul!" she squeals. She squeezes him into her bosom, her eyes gleaming and filled with joy. I laugh out loud at his mortified expression as he tries to pull away. Beside me, I hear Janine snort too. I had almost forgotten she was there. I clear my throat anxiously.

"Happy birthday, Paul." Janine says as we all sit around the table.

"Cheers," he says through a mouthful of cake. "It was yesterday though." Ma beams at us as she vigorously scrubs a counter. I swear, she never stops cleaning.

Paul's face is glum.

"Why are you sad?" I ask. He shrugs me off.

"Go on, tell us!" Bea butts in. Paul looks slightly surprised; I doubt he'd noticed this stranger in his house until this moment. Coming to a conclusion, he replies huskily,

"My mates in the city ditched me ." I overhear Janine mutter something under her breath about him being a bit of a baby.

"Oh," I say, not wanting to embarrass him by laughing. Ma seems aghast at learning this though.

"What? How could they? What happened?!" she demands, slamming down her dish cloth, her twitchy brown eyes alive with displeasure. Paul shrugs indifferently.

"They're all on holiday, or off with girlfriends, or something. It's boring by yourself," he complains.

"Well, love," Ma continues, taking a couple of deep breaths. "It's alright. Me and Pa have got you a very nice birthday present, Paulie. Maybe that'll cheer you up."

He perks up slightly. "What did you get me, Ma?"

Ma runs out of the room delightedly and returns a few seconds later with a jangling set of keys waving in her hand. For a moment, Paul doesn't react. Then, fully realising what this is, he jumps up.

"A *car*, Ma?" he gasps, the breathless shock and joy painted on his face. Ma looks like she might cry with happiness.

"Yes, Paulie!"

For the first time ever, I see Paul willingly hug Ma. It's quite a scene.

Winnie seems to agree. "Wow," she says, her voice slightly dipped in sarcasm.

"I know, it's so nice," Bea replies soppily, completely misunderstanding Winnie.

Paul spends the rest of the day letting Pa teach him how to drive. Even he is a little jaunty, because he's used to driving his trusty old tractor – a much larger and heavier piece of machinery. But slowly, they're both getting to know how to let the flashy red car slide smoothly across the road. In fact, Paul seems to think he's ready to pass his driver's test, and tries to convince Pa to sign him up for driving lessons right away. Pa chuckles and scratches his grey wisps of hair.

"Paulie, lad, your ma and I aren't *made* of money."

Paul is distressed. "So how am I meant to learn to drive then?"

"I'll teach you," Pa tells him seriously. Ma, bustling towards him to give him his drink, tuts loudly.

"Is that a safe decision, dear?" she asks warily. Pa waves her off, like she's an irritable fly, waiting to be swatted away.

"Well, you're a clever boy, aren't you?" Pa continues. Paul nods uncertainly; Ma leaps to life.

"Of course he is, he got such brilliant exam results, didn't you, love?"

Hesitantly, Paul nods again. "Well, I could've done better, but–"

"Oh, Paulie, you were practically the best in the class!" Ma interrupts.

I stare at my brother, eyes wide. He shakes his head quickly.

"Ma, you're exaggerating a bit, I think." Paul attempts, scratching at the back of his neck nervously. I doubt she even hears him.

"I'm trying to say that it's won't take much for you to learn how to drive, will it now?" Pa says. Paul doesn't reply.

Bored of watching them, I amble inside the house. I hadn't finished my slice of cake earlier today, before all my friends left, and I spoon up some of it now thoughtfully. It's six in the afternoon already. Ma will be cooking dinner soon; there's no point in calling at Janine's house to see if she can come back outside.

There's a loud cheer from outside.

"Attaboy!" Pa exclaims. I peer out the window.

"Did I do it? Did I change the gears right?" Paul says in disbelief.

"I told you you're clever!" Ma cries triumphantly.

"Didn't I say that?" Pa says, puzzled. No one answers him.

Days of Paul relentlessly showing off pass in the blink of an eye. Soon enough, it's the day before the summer festival. Funnily enough, my brother is doing exactly the same thing – practicing his driving and begging Pa to sign him up for proper lessons – when I leave the house that morning to go to call round at Janine's as usual. I thought things between us would be a little spiky after that weird hug, but I seem to have been the only one to have put such significance on it. For some reason, this makes me a bit disappointed.

"Hi," I say as she comes out, bang on time. I hear her ma yell something after her, but Janine slams the door shut.

"What was that about?" I ask gingerly. She frowns and stares at the ground.

"Her stupid sponge cake that she'd made for the festival thing didn't rise properly in the oven," she replies, kicking the dust with her shoe.

"You don't usually argue," I remark. She laughs.

"No, we don't. She's normally the peacemaker and I'm normally the one that gets angry!"

I smile.

"Hello," Winnie's voice startles me.

"Oh, hey." I say.

"Hi!" Janine exclaims excitedly. Winnie hadn't been able to get out yesterday, and they're both chuffed to see each other now. So chuffed, actually, that Winnie isn't dripping all over me like a melting ice cream, which I make a personal note of to thank God for tomorrow at church.

21

Winnie

The first person I notice when I step out of the house is Cameron, chatting to Janine, his hair like liquid gold in the sun. I blink in the bright light until I've adjusted to it. Janine looks grumpy. Maybe it's because she missed me yesterday. Mother needed my help; she says she's been feeling really ill recently and she can't bear to do the housework alone. I thought maybe she was lying, although Mother has never lied to me in her life – but I heard her retching in the bathroom, and when she emerged her expression was sick and watery. She went to lie down after that, and I finished the chores by myself.

The summer festival is tomorrow, and I'm very excited for it. Mother has finished making me a skirt with beautifully-sewn sequins; though her recent illness had been slowing her down a little, so I helped too and it's gorgeous. This will be my first time going because Father never trusted me to go out by myself before, but he says I'm old enough now. I can't wait.

"Hello," I say, startling both Cameron and Janine.

"Winnie!" says Janine, rushing up to me. Cameron backs away uneasily, seeming to be a bit wary of me. I'm so pleased with Janine's reaction though that I decide I don't care.

22

Cameron

Ma's positively buzzing with energy for the summer festival tomorrow. She volunteered to help out with food and decorations, which leaves me a few extra responsibilities around the farm as she's so busy, but I don't mind. Each morning these past couple of days, I've been tending to Ma's chickens; collecting eggs, cleaning their nesting boxes, feeding them grains. Each morning, they peck me like crazy, because they're used to Ma, not me. It doesn't really hurt, but it makes me feel a bit rejected.

When I haven't been doing chores, I've been subtly leaving the house to meet up with Janine and Winnie and Bea. They're all really excited too. Winnie keeps bragging about what she's going to wear, and Bea listens, wide-eyed, maybe a bit jealous.

"Mother has been sewing it for me," Winnie says proudly. She pauses and adds, "Well, actually, I've been doing some of it myself. She's been feeling terribly nauseous lately. Maybe it's because she's eating so much more."

"What does nauseous mean?" Bea asks chirpily. No one replies to her.

"...Why is she eating so much more?" Janine asks, grinning. "What if she gets fat?"

I wait for Winnie to get upset, but she smiles back at Janine and gets that it's a joke.

"When we had Daisy – the cow we had before Dolly – she had a calf and she gained a lot of weight and got really round," I chip in without thinking. Winnie scowls at me. Janine looks worried for a second, but she changes the topic and there's no argument. I don't know why I said that. I didn't mean to compare her ma to a cow. I have a feeling that if she disliked me, she wouldn't have dropped the subject so easily.

23

Janine

It's Friday afternoon – *the* Friday afternoon: it's the day of the summer festival. Mum seems to be more desperate than ever to win that china tea set. I can't fathom why; she doesn't even really like drinking tea.

"Just a nice cup of black coffee for me," she always says. I don't get that either. Coffee is disgusting – so dark and bitter and horribly grainy – so I just don't understand why she would want to take away the sweet milk and make it even worse. I had a sip out of her mug once; never again. She came back in the room to find me wiping my tongue vigorously with a napkin.

Right now, Mum is baking at a furious, break-neck speed, whizzing around the kitchen like she has wheels for feet. Flour flies around the room – there's some of it in Mum's hair too, but she doesn't even seem to care.

There's suddenly a knock at the door. Intrigued, I open it to find Bea smiling at me sunnily.

"Hi," I say, not quite understanding.

"Hiya!" she exclaims, squeezing me so tight I think I might suffocate.

"What is it, do you want to go out?" I wheeze after slowly pulling away from her.

She rolls her eyes at me and, placing a hand on my shoulder, shakes me playfully. However, it's a violent convulsion for my bony body and I almost fall over.

"Well, the festival starts in a bit, silly!" she says.

"I know," I stare at her, nibbling my lip. "Are you sure you're allowed to go, Bea?"

A flash of a hurt expression pulses on her face. "No," she says.

"Oh," I say. She hasn't been allowed out at all anyway, but it will be harder to keep her out for so long and so late without her grandma finding out. "Well," I start hopefully. "Of course we can still sneak you out, your grandma will never know. Don't worry."

It'll be fine.

About an hour later, the clock shudders to six and I glance outside for the millionth time, more jittery than I'm ready to admit. I'm waiting for Cameron and Paul with his car – Paul insisted, though we can walk there in twenty-five minutes – to come so we can head to the festival. Mum is cradling her pretty pink box of cinnamon buns (that's what she decided on in the end) and I smooth over my frilly skirt obsessively. It won't make it any less ridiculously bouncy, but Mum forced me to wear it, and I've learnt not to argue so much with her. I don't know – before we moved to the countryside, I was with her all day, every day, and yes, we survived, but I guess we got a little sick of each other. Now I'm barely in the house for the most part of the day.

"Janine!" Mum says, tapping my shoulder. She cocks her head towards the window, and my eyes follow her gaze. Paul toots the horn of his flashy red car and, seeing me through the window, calls out boisterously,

"Come on!"

Looking closer, I spot Cameron fastened tightly in the back seat, peering around apprehensively. I smile and beckon to Mum to come outside with me. Her lipstick is dynamically red – a matte, crimson glue on her lips that shines like a bright red-hot beacon when she smiles. She smiles often too: as we wait for Winnie to come out, Mum seems to be constantly beaming.

At last, Winnie saunters out of her house. She really does look lovely – she's wearing a long, draping skirt adorned with sequins that sparkle in the afternoon sun, and a tiny, smart white top that makes her perfect teeth seem whiter still. She flaunts and flutters her dress about like a butterfly, dancing in the street. Winnie loves every moment of attention.

A few minutes later, Bea has sneaked out, and she looks pretty dressed up as well. She's wearing a light, flower-printed dress that seems to billow out like a rose when she walks. When you look up close, you can see that it's actually a little ragged, but Bea's smile makes up for any plainness in her attire.

Every so often, I glance at Cameron, who is unusually quiet.

"Do you guys like my dress?" she proudly asks everyone at one point. Mum gushes all over her, showering her with compliments – I know for a fact that she doesn't mean most of it – while Winnie assures her she looks great, flicking her long skirt smugly. Paul, to no one's surprise, completely ignores her, as I smile and say it's really nice. Cameron, the only one who hasn't said anything, shrugs.

"Are you alright?" I ask him quietly. He nods hurriedly, then really thinks about it.

"I don't know, I just feel a bit... off. Don't worry, it's fine," he falters and looks away. I leave him alone. Bea is oblivious though, and happily gazes into the clouds. Yes, there are clouds in the sky: it's sort of disheartening, because we've had so many clear days. Now, the clouds clot over the sun a little, like small puffs of cotton. The air, though, is humid and sort of suffocating this afternoon, and I notice this while the others talk about how we should get to the festival. I stand there awkwardly on the side, not really listening to what they're saying.

"I can only fit four people in the car." Paul is saying, starting to look annoyed.

"Well, you can take Janine, her ma, Winnie and Bea and then come back for me." Cameron says decisively. At this suggestion, Paul raises his eyebrows at him scornfully.

"Aww, look at you, you gentleman, letting the ladies go first!" he says, his voice mocking and a little spiteful. Cameron goes cherry-red and his eyes shoot to his slightly scuffed Sunday best shoes. Feeling bad for him, I try to catch his eye but his gaze is now firmly glued to the ground.

I would've expected Mum to be at Paul's throat for that remark; she certainly would've been at mine if I dreamed of saying that to one of my friends in front of her. Perplexingly, she just seems a little taken aback, and remarks, her voice gentle, but firm:

"Well, that was rude." Paul stubbornly ignores this and doesn't even look at her, but I know he heard her and he looks a little bit embarrassed now. I doubt he'll make fun of Cameron in front of Mum again.

"That could work, though," Mum continues, addressing everyone now. "You know, what Cameron said."

"Yes," Winnie says slowly – she clearly disagrees but her strict parents taught her not to ever talk back to an adult. "It-it could work… but how about if you, Ma'am, and Janine, Cameron and I went together?"

"Well, what about Bea?" Mum asks.

Ah. Winnie seems to be acting territorial again.

"Paul can come round a second time and drive her over then." Winnie says, trying to keep the whine out of her voice.

Mum isn't convinced. I've noticed that she seems to like Bea a lot, and it's bizarre, because Mum is the witty, charming Gina: Bea is a simple girl from the countryside. Yet, somehow, I catch Mum gazing fondly at her every now and then. It's quite puzzling.

While I'm lost in these thoughts, everyone else seems to have come to a decision.

"Right, so," Paul is saying, all prim and business-like. "I've got Cam, Winnie and, um," he gestures to Bea, seeming to have forgotten her name again.

"Bea," she says, totally unfazed.

"Alright," Paul says. I doubt he even listened to her. He's like that, Paul – he doesn't try to hurt people, he's just a little ignorant, I suppose. To be honest, I'm not sure that puts him in a much better light.

Suddenly, all of what he'd been saying sinks in. "Wait!" I cry. "Why can't we come?"

"Only four seats," Paul replies wearily. "I'm pretty sure I've said that about a hundred–"

"I can still come, and you can take my Mum the second time around!"

Mum scowls at me. "Will you stop it, Janine?!"

And so it goes on. I zone out eventually, too tired of it to make any sort of contribution, but I watch Bea and Cameron and Winnie intently. Bea isn't really paying attention to anything that's going on either. Her eyes are fixed on an angel-white butterfly as it dances in the sun. Cameron is starting to look uneasy with all the quarrelling, but he daren't interrupt his brother Paul. Winnie goggles her great big moony eyes at all the action, parting her mouth open every now and then to say something but never getting any words out.

I flicker my eyes away from them and zone back into the conversation. "Please, Mum, can I go with my friends?" I beg. I can't stand being left behind; it makes me feel like I'm on the outside. It's no use, though. Their minds are made up now and everything has been decided.

I watch as they clamber excitedly into the car, with Mum's cold hand on my shoulder, like she's worried I might try to run off.

"Can't we just walk there? Surely, it can't take longer than twenty minutes to get to the festival?" I ask her irritably. Mum just shakes her head solemnly, not really looking at me.

"Paul wants to drive us." she says simply.

I let out an annoyed *humph*.

"He wants to feel important," she continues, although I didn't really expect her to elaborate. I don't reply; I'm not quite sure if she wants me to, or if she's really talking to me at all. The way her eyes are fixated on a vague, faraway point in the distance makes me wonder if she's talking to herself. Dragging my eyes away from Mum, I try to find what she's looking at, following her line of sight. She seems to be staring at the road Paul zoomed down a few minutes ago with my friends with his crimson car. Mum seems to be looking further than that, though, which is impossible, because the furthest you can see is where the road turns a swift corner. Maybe she's not looking there at all, I ponder. Maybe she's not really looking anywhere at all.

We stand there in silence for a few minutes before suddenly, without either of us expecting it, Paul actually appears, the sun bouncing off the glamorous red roof. He toots his horn expectantly, but we've already seen him. I wave, trying to smile. I should be really happy now; I *am* happy. I'm going to the summer festival! It's going to be so much fun... I feel a wave of glee swallow me up and I find I can't stand still.

"Come on, Mum!" I say, grinning, pulling on her hand like a small toddler. She smiles at me. Maybe she's seeing the small toddler in me too.

Paul gets out of the car and attempts a toothy grin himself.

"In you get," he says to me, opening the car door to the back seats. They seem to be made of plush leather, though it's slightly cracked in places; I know Paul and Cameron's mum and dad can't really afford a posh new car, so this is second-hand. Mum tries to get in with me, but Paul insists on her staying in the front with him. It doesn't take much persuasion, to be fair; Mum wants to feel like a princess.

"Is your seatbelt on, Janine?" Mum asks me anxiously as Paul is about to set off. I had completely forgotten about it.

"One moment," I say briefly, trying to get it on. It seems too tight, too restricted; I can hardly get it to click in the clasp. At last, it's in though... or so I think. Thirty seconds later, it slides back off. I don't bother to slip it back on, though. Paul is shooting along the roads now, trying to impress us, I suppose. I can't say it isn't working – I roll down the window and stick my head out. It's the most wonderful feeling. My hair is totally messed up from the wind, sticking up precisely where it shouldn't, so I look a bit like a bird's nest, but I couldn't care less. It's so fast! There isn't even any wind today, but the car zooms past so fast, you'd think you're riding a cheetah. Throwing back my head with the window still wide open, I let the wind ruffle my skirt, get in my top and fluff out, in my hair, in my mouth…

"Ha!" I cry out happily without meaning to. However, it attracts Mum's attention and she spins around.

"Janine! Look at you, you look a mess!" she groans, looking from my hair to my ruffled skirt and the now slightly crinkled top that isn't so neatly tucked in anymore. Not that I care remotely – I clench my jaw firmly though to stop myself from arguing with Mum, though, as she starts to fuss and fret over me. Seeing me looking so solemn and serious, she stops and says with a touch of concern in her voice,

"What's the matter? *Smile*, darling."

Paul, turning back for just a second, adds teasingly, "Yes, darling, do smile!"

My eyes shoot daggers at him and Mum pretends to be very cross, but I know that she isn't really. Even I can't help grinning when he continues with,

"Right. We're almost there now, darlings."

Then, quite suddenly, the car slows down to a child's pace, and Paul stops all teasing, all childish behaviour whatsoever, because a gaggle of teenage girls is watching the car – watching *him* – and giggling, flirting. I see a hint of a grin that reaches to his ears from my seat in the back, and the girls all scream with laughter. Paul refuses to be fazed, though, and continues to smile charmingly. He's so pathetic. Even Mum lets out a frenzied snort.

"Paul, hurry up please, we'll be late," she says gently. Taking one last goggle-eyed stare at the girls, he accelerates. However, it's exceptionally bad timing, because we swerve wildly around a corner. I lurch to the side crazily and bang my head hard on the window. Just in front of me, Mum yells out and tries to grab my hand, but we can't quite reach each other properly. *She* hasn't really moved from her seat at all, unlike me, but she's shaking now. And at the wheel, Paul is still trying to regain control of the car. Without warning, it slides to the side again, almost crashing into a nearby lamppost. This time, I tumble to the ground. Mum shrieks again.

"Paul!" she says.

"I'm trying!" he shouts back. We slide forward this time. I bash my nose so hard on Mum seat, I'm sure it's bleeding.

"Ow..." I moan softly.

"Darling!–" Mum reassures me desperately as Paul swerves to avoid hitting a tree.

But it's not my nose that has my attention right now. When I fell to the floor, I landed so clumsily, with my elbow right in the crook of the car door handle, that I must have opened it somehow. My elbow must be bruised. None of that matters right now.

The car door swings open! I scream. My hand clutches at the leather, the seat, the door, the... anything, anything that I could hold on to. But my fingers slip off like they're coated in slime. And now I'm falling. Falling. Falling to the ground.

24

Cameron

Where is she? Winnie and Bea and I have been standing around and waiting for ages now. The drive only took a few minutes for us. What's taking Paul so long?

Other people are arriving too in small bubbly groups, chatting and laughing. There are stalls set up with snacks and Ma's brought some of her jewellery too, which always does well at the festival. She's already here too, bustling about busily. Music suddenly blurts out from a speaker somewhere, and soon the entire scene is joyful and lively.

Winnie looks around excitedly, taking it all in. For some reason, I don't feel in the party mood. She tries to meet my eyes but I know that she'll suggest joining in with the festival and letting Janine find us herself whenever she arrives, so I look the other way. Bea, who is normally just as curious and enthusiastic, is unusually subdued. She's probably thinking about her Gran. Maybe she feels guilty for leaving when she knew she wasn't allowed. I'm starting to feel uneasy that I didn't insist on Janine coming on the journey with us. Paul's probably being ridiculous and annoying. Maybe he met up with mates and that's what's taking them so long. Maybe Janine and her ma are being held up by Paul. Maybe they got fed up and they're walking here. Maybe that's it. Pa caught him at his whiskey this morning. He hadn't been drinking it, I think. He's not that stupid. I hope not.

25

Janine

My eyes are screwed shut, so I don't see anything when I land. I'm so braced that I barely *feel* anything when I fall.

I sob hard.

"Mum!" I shout, my eyes still firmly closed. It's so quiet. It's so cold.

"Mum," I say again weakly, opening my eyes now to look around. Oh... oh. Everything is on its side. Paul's red car is halted, left messily a few metres away from where I am. I can taste the vomit in the back of my throat.

My eyes are still open; I look around slowly, trying to see the rest of my body. My fists are still clenched – I unfurl them stiffly to see pale, sweaty hands; pale, sweaty arms. They're pale and they're sweaty, but they are OK. It doesn't hurt to move them. I turn to my legs. Looking down at them is somewhat difficult, because I'm lying down, but my stomach does a somersault when I see them. One of my legs seems to be now bent at an ugly angle. Or maybe my tears are blurring everything out of proportion. All I know is that my legs hurt. And I can't move them.

"Mum, my legs..." I manage to mumble. The moment I've breathed the words out, I have to close my eyes to steady myself, because a searing pain shoots in the back of my head.

"Oh my God, Janine..." she cries, suddenly running to my side. Her figure looms over me. I breathe shakily in and out, trying to calm the throbbing in my skull.

"Legs," I whisper, swallowing hard to stop the tears from spilling.

90

I see Paul get out of the car a few metres away; he puts his head in his hands in complete despair. Mum is trembling so hard next that she almost collapses on the paved ground. I let out a broken sob. Why are they so scared?

Acting on instinct, Paul rushes forward and stares, just stares at me. There's a knot in the back of my throat. His eyes wide as saucers, Paul slowly backs away again, a hand clasped around his mouth. Unsure of what to do, I lie there helplessly like a broken doll.

"Mum, help me get up," I say through tears. She just stands there, staring at me in horror as if I've been torn apart, limb from limb. More worried than before, I hurriedly try to check myself over to make sure there really isn't any blood, but it hurts so badly when I try to lift my neck that I let it rest back on the pavement. The world spins again and I see little white stars everywhere.

I gulp. "Mum, I can't get up," I whisper.

Silence seems to stretch out. I can't quite see Mum's face from my angle. I prick my ears in anticipation, expecting someone to walk past; children playing, people returning from work, locals heading to the festivals, anyone. Mum is still eerily quiet.

"Mum?" I try again. Instead, Paul approaches me, also morosely silent. Before I realise what he intends to do, he is grabbing my arm, so hard that his fingers leave marks in my skin. I think he's trying to help me get up.

"Stop!" Mum bellows, leaping to life, pushing him out of the way. "Don't touch her, you could seriously hurt her! Look at her!"

Paul is aghast. "I know, it was my fault, I'm so sorry–"

"Call an ambulance!" she exclaims.

"Right." He says, his face pale and sickly. He pauses. "How?"

Mum looks ready to strangle him. She breathes deeply and looks around. "Look, see, Paul, there's a little corner shop down the road. Ask to use a telephone there." Looking back at me and Mum one last time, he starts to run shakily. He looks as if he'd break down in tears any moment.

Trying to ignore his panic, I call out to Mum again.

"Mum," I say, trying to keep my voice from wobbling. "Mum, help me get up please."

"No, darling, I can't do that," she says firmly, watching Paul as he tries to speed-walk back to us with his gangly legs; she comes to sit beside me. I reach out with my hand to squeeze hers, but she jumps and scolds me.

"You mustn't move, you silly girl!" she stops and holds her face in her hands. Then she peeks up at me again and croaks, "Oh, I'm sorry, Janine. I'm sorry. I'm sorry."

It's sort of absurd, because my arms are absolutely fine, but she scares me a little and I obediently lower my hand to the ground. I feel trapped – trapped in a shell, in a soldier's armour that restricts my movement, restricts my breathing, makes me gasp for air, makes me long for a way out of the pain. And then... it comes.

Slowly, dreadfully slowly, I feel the pain all melt away: in my legs, it ebbs away like stormy raindrops slipping off a leaf; in my head, it seems to weigh me down, sinking me further and further into the cemented road until I'm sure I'm buried beneath it all. It feels like my whole body is shutting down, pulling down the blinds... and with that, I close my eyes. And now I can't hear anything. Mum's voice fades away. At one point, there's a distant siren coming towards us and as if I'm in a dream, I feel vague, unfamiliar hands lifting me up. Are these the angels? Am I going to heaven? Mum and I have never really been religious, but maybe this is what it's really like after you die.

◆

Part 2

1

Winnie

It's all so bitter. The holidays felt pointless. They were endless. I kept replaying the night of the summer festival: the incessant waiting; their unnerving absence the whole evening; the gut-wrenching dread that something truly awful had happened as we wandered back home.

The next morning, we all found out. Cameron and Bea and I saw Janine's mother at the market. She looked an absolute mess, with tufts of her auburn hair sticking up this way and that, and dark circles under blue eyes that were still alive as ever despite an overall slightly zombie-like appearance. She spotted us almost immediately, and told us everything. I still remember that horrified look on Cameron's face. We all already knew what had happened by that point, so his emotional reaction surprised me. He told me later though that it was a lot more painful to hear it directly from Janine's mother. He said it made it more real. I still don't think that it's completely registered in my head what's happened; I wake up sometimes and think about going outside with Janine, about where we could go today and the games we could play. When I remember, it feels like a blow and suddenly my head is pierced with pain and I have to stop thinking about it.

It's colder outside now. The clouds wrap themselves around our little green bubble like dreary grey serpents. Everything feels muffled.

2

Bea

Gran's getting worse. I can feel it. Somehow, I feel like it's all my fault. I told her about the summer festival in the end. I had to. When I got back, she was already awake, sitting upright in her bed, waiting for me. She said she wasn't angry, and I believed her – she was disappointed. Maybe she was a bit shocked too. Maybe this sudden uproar of emotion caused her to take a turn for the worse. Although I felt immensely guilty, it gave me hope, seeing her so much stronger that night; we hadn't talked properly in a long time, and even though I was told off, I was so grateful for it.

3

Janine

"She appears unconscious," a voice said gruffly. I remember hazily trying to open my eyes and to my shock, seeing that I was lying in some small sort of room, with people surrounding me. They were wearing crinkled uniforms and one was now frowning at me anxiously. For one dazed moment, I thought they were angels.

"She's awake!" he called sharply. The other two huddled close by.

A woman started: "Janine, I'm a doctor, I'm going to help you get better, but I need you to stay with us now, don't go back to sleep, don't close your eyes…"

But the sound of her voice was already fading away.

"Wake up, please, wake up!" the woman said, gently but with urgency in her voice.

Suddenly, there was a brisk movement and everything seems to skid to the right. I realised with a jolt that we weren't in a room, we were in an ambulance. I wasn't dead at all. The doctors were going to make me all better. Trying to sit up now, I mumbled,

"Where's my mum?"

"She'll be at the hospital with your brother, dear, you'll see them soon–"

"He's not my brother!" I said furiously, realising with a gutted feeling in my stomach that they must have been talking about Paul. This was all his fault, anyway. If he hadn't been showing off, the accident would never have happened.

The rest of that day was frustratingly blurry. I saw Mum and Paul when we got to the hospital, but the doctors wouldn't let me stay with her. Then I remember a needle which made everything feel like wading through a pool of knee-deep treacle… it was like a dream; the harder I pushed, the slower I went. After that, everything is faded. My memories of that day often merge with other days, because staying at the hospital was incredibly monotonous and repetitive, so the weeks all merged into one big muddled mess. I felt completely lost.

The doctor that took care of me was called Dr Philips, and he was sort of disgusting. Whenever he would talk to me, he would lean his face in so close that I could count his nose hairs. It makes me grimace just remembering.

I much preferred the wrinkled, smiley nurse in the blue scrubs, who would visit the ward every morning, grinning and pushing a food trolley. The food itself was disappointing: cheese sandwiches that tasted like cardboard and bland little pots of rice pudding.

The doctor was an abrupt, no-nonsense sort of man, but he was so horribly careful and pitying of me when he broke the news. I remember him chuckling uncomfortably and clearing his throat, and telling Mum and I about how it will take months to heal the injuries, and mentioning names of bones that I don't know, and talking about possible nerve damage. Mum's frown darkened as he spoke but when I caught her eye, she smiled warmly at me, as though absolutely nothing was happening. When Dr Philips, scratching the back of his head with one pale, hairy hand, cautiously acknowledged the fact that it was possible to not make a full recovery, and that in this case I would not regain full mobility in my legs, Mum was devastated.

"I'm sorry, Ma'am," he said, scrunching up his nose a little and swivelling back around to see Mum's horror-stricken face. "I'm sorry, but I must tell you the truth." And he sauntered out of the room without another word.

There were a few seconds of silence before I heard a little sob from Mum.

"Mum," I said, trying to sit up again so I could comfort her.

"Oh! Careful, doll." The nurse said quietly, walking slowly towards Mum and reaching for one of her hands. "Let's take this outside, ma'am," the nurse murmured. They walked out slowly. I couldn't see them, but although their voices were hushed, I could still hear snippets of what they were saying.

"Ma'am..." the nurse said gently.

Mum snuffled. "Gina, please... Call me Gina."

"Gina...all be fine."

I heard Mum gulp. "How ...?" she said. "If Janine doesn't recover..."

The nurse's tone was so gentle and soft that I had to strain my ears . "Gina... Janine ... absolutely fine."

"But what if ... doesn't recover? Oh my God... Can't move her legs for the rest of her *life*? Oh my God..." The nurse said nothing.

"Oh my God..." Mum repeated, breaking down in tears again.

The nurse sighed softly. "Gina... she started. "Dr Philips ... very skilled doctor."

Mum cried harder still, and my heart felt like it was breaking.

"Gina," the nurse continued. "... Will do everything he possibly can..."

Mum was silent. I could almost feel her looking at me from the hallway, and I tried to look as though I wasn't listening.

"I know... Thank you." she sniffed.

The nurse sighed. "It's true... possible that Janine ... not be able to regain full mobility in her legs," she said slowly, but so clearly that I caught most of it. Mum was deadly quiet.

My breath caught in my throat. I had hoped that maybe pompous old Dr Philips was just exaggerating.

"But ... firmly believe ... Janine ... fight through it," the nurse said. "Many, many people ...learn to ... with ... disabilities ... have wonderful, fulfilled lives, even if ... certain things they cannot do."

I stared at the ceiling, piecing it all together. I hadn't thought about that. It hit me then that I might not be able to run, to skip, to swim, to climb…

"… So many things … disabled people *can* do," the nurse added enthusiastically. Mum still hadn't said anything. I wondered how she was taking all of this.

The nurse said very quietly, "And Janine… very brave girl. Either way … will be fine."

I thought about this for long after their conversation has ended.

The next few weeks are torture. I'm constantly confined to my bed like a prisoner. I have to just lie flat on the bed and not to worry, there's a good girl, Janine. At first, they don't even let me sit up, and when they do, I'm supervised like I might suddenly decide to run away, which stings, because I can't run away, can I?

The first few days are so lonely. I only see Nurse Adams and that gross Dr Philips. Well, Mum too; she's always with me. Often, I wake up in the morning to find her fast asleep on the chair next to my bed.

But after a little while, they move me to a part of the hospital just for children called the girls ward. It's sort of strange to see that there are other people that are going through the same thing as me. Actually, most of the girls are a lot younger than me. There's one moody teenage girl that refuses to talk to anyone, but the rest are all still in primary school. There's one little girl, Betty, who's just four. I sometimes watch her with her mum and grandma when they read her storybooks – she always claps her hands delightedly and laughs and grins from ear to ear. Her mum and grandma laugh along, but her mum's eyes often go shiny with tears. `

I'm never that happy. In fact, I scarcely ever smile anymore. Mum is always, always bright and hopeful, but now that just annoys me. I can't help being like this now. I can't make myself get better. Oh, I wish I could. Sometimes I daydream about just getting up and running out of here, but it always leads to tears, because no matter how hard I try, I can never do it.

Dr Philips is an ignorant old bum, but Nurse Adams was right, he *does* know what he's doing. And he *does* seem to have hopes of me making a proper recovery, but he never seems too excited about it. It's like he doesn't want us to be hopeful.

Nurse Adams tried to explain to me once that he's not trying to be mean; he just doesn't want us to be disappointed if it doesn't happen. I told her that that's stupid. How can we not be hopeful? And how can we not be disappointed if it does end like that? Then I blew a big raspberry in her face and crossed my arms. That was really horrible of me, but sometimes I can't help it. I get so angry and frustrated with everything and everyone that I say all sorts of spiteful things. Even to Mum. Frequently, I ignore her completely if she's trying to talk to me. She gets very sad, and it makes me feel terrible. But she doesn't tell me off. It's like I'm too fragile to risk upsetting. Well, *that* makes me feel worse still. I don't want to be pitied like that. No. No! I almost wish that I were being properly disciplined for all the horrid things I say.

There are no good days. There are no days when I don't upset anyone, there are no days when I don't cry myself silly, there are no days when I don't wish I were anyone but me. I hate how I have to live now. Everything is so horribly awkward: from the disgusting toileting rituals that I have to endure every day with my dear Nurse Adams, my cheeks flaming hot, to the physiotherapy with Dr Philips: the sweaty, heavy work of learning to manoeuvre my legs around by myself. I can feel my legs, we've all established that, but it's like I've forgotten how to move them. They're surprisingly heavy too; these two skinny, stick-like little legs.

A few days ago, Dr Philips got me a wheelchair. It's actually pretty cool, but I didn't tell anyone that. Instead, I didn't talk to anyone and sat there grumpily until they gave up and went away, leaving the wheelchair next to the bed. After a few more minutes of sulking, I decided to abandon all my pride and all my ego and I shouted for Nurse Adams.

"Nurse! Nurse Adams!" I cried. A couple of seconds later, she came running, looking flustered.

"Janine! Is everything alright? Did you hurt yourself, my sweet?"

I shook my head adamantly, casting a side-long glance at the wheelchair. The nurse saw this, and after some consideration, pushed it a few inches closer to me.

"Pretty cool, don't you think?" she said playfully, smiling at me. I remained strangely quiet.

"You know..." the nurse continued coyly. "If I didn't know you better, I'd think that you might actually want to try it out,"

I stared at her, expressionless.

After a small pause, she said, "... Do you?"

And it turned out that she was absolutely right. I did.

I'll spare you the awkward details of when she had to carry me out of the bed and into the chair, but once I was settled in, I must admit that it felt sort of powerful. I know, that's really strange – I was even smaller than I am drawn at my full height, but I suppose there's something about wheels that gets my attention.

Oh. Wow. No, actually, that's not completely accurate, because every time I think of Paul's red car, of the skidding wheels, of the door flying open, I...

But anyway, Nurse Adams pushed me all around the girls' ward, and then outside a little in the corridors. It was a little frustrating that I couldn't do it by myself – after all, how hard could it be to wheel myself around? I'm only a little titch – but the nurse insisted that I'm not yet strong enough, and that was that. But overall, it was the most fun I'd had for a long time.

This morning, I woke up at about eight to the sight of a big pink bouquet of flowers on my bedside table, which was a pleasant surprise, and I wondered who had sent them, and the sound of crying from the little four-year-old girl, Betty, which was pretty normal. She must've had another nightmare. She has *loads*; sometimes, she wets the bed, too.

There was no one in the room, not even Nurse Adams, who's almost always with us, so I quietly called out for Betty to try and comfort her. This made the poor thing sob harder still. I looked over, and there was Mum, fast asleep in the chair next to my bed, a cold cup of tea cradled in one hand.

"Mum," I said softly. "Mum!"

She jerked awake, nearly spilling her chilled tea, and when she saw the situation, she gave me a fond smile and slowly walked up to Betty's bed.

"It's OK," she murmured, sitting down on the edge of the bed. "Shh, it was only a bad dream... only a bad dream, baby..."

Eventually, Betty was gently lulled back to sleep, and Mum came ambling back to me. With one smooth white hand, she reached out to me and tickled my nose.

"You're such a good girl," she whispered, and then sank back into the chair, falling back asleep too.

4

Winnie

"Winnie, what happened to Janine?" Bea asks me one afternoon as we walk home after school. The sole of one of her shoes is starting to peel off, and flaps against the ground every time she lifts her foot.

"She hurt her legs in the accident, Bea," I tell her wearily.

"Is it my fault?"

I scoff. "No, of course not!" I pause, remembering what we know from what Paul and Janine's mother had told us of what happened. "Cameron's brother crashed the car," I say quietly, trying to be discreet.

"It is my fault!" she insists, speaking quietly at first then increasing to piercing cries, holding her head in her hands in despair. "It's my fault...and Gran's fault..."

I halt. "What? Your grandmother? What does she have to do with anything?"

"I saw her at the festival," Bea gabbles. "In the crowd, maybe looking for me..."

This is shocking. "You saw your grandmother at the festival way back in June?"

Bea nods quickly. I suck my teeth sceptically.

"You told us that she's ill. You said she can't even get up out of bed. You're a liar."

"She is ill!" she protests. "She can't get out of bed! I didn't lie!"

"Then you're lying now," I say accusingly.

"No I'm not! I promise, I saw her there, I'm not a liar!"

"I don't believe you. You're trying to trick me."

103

"Why would I–"

"I don't know, but why would your grandmother be there? It makes no sense. You're a liar, and a bad one too." The words pour out of me like poison before I can stop them.

"I'm not, I'm not, I'm not a liar!" she says hysterically, her eyes looking like they'll pop out of their sockets.

I don't say anything. It's quiet for a few moments but for the sound of Bea's rapid, pant-like breathing, and the rhythmic flapping of the soles of her shoes.

"I'm not lying, I promise, she was there," she says finally.

"Why… why would your grandmother be there?"

"Winnie, I'm not lying, I promise–"

"–Alright, alright, fine, but why was she there then? What was your grandmother doing at the festival?"

Bea swallows. She hesitates before saying, "That's why it's all my fault."

I stop for a second, deciding to take a kinder approach. "Bea, look, what happened to Janine wasn't your fault,"

She breathes in shakily. "It was. I don't know what Gran was doing at the festival, but she must have seen me, a-and she must've realised that I snuck out without her knowing, a-and she decided to punish me…"

My face sets into a grim expression. She's right. There's no point trying to be kind. "She decided to punish you by cursing Janine," I say. I half-expect Bea to burst into tears, but I think she'd gotten there a long time ago. I feel a short pang of sympathy for her – she must be so frightened of her grandmother. I can't really blame her for being related to a witch, I suppose.

"Since… since the festival," Bea starts, her voice wobbly. "Since the festival, Gran has taken a turn for the worse."

"You mean, she's sicker?"

Bea nods uncomfortably.

I consider this. "I suppose her dark spell on Janine must have sapped her of her energy,"

"I hadn't thought of that. You're right," Bea says, her pale hazel eyes burning into mine. It strikes me then that this is the first proper conversation we've had since we met.

5

Cameron

Ma was livid. She wouldn't speak to Paul for weeks after Janine's accident. At first, if they stumbled upon each other in the same room, Ma would make a big show of storming off furiously, leaving him bomb shelled and stricken. The truth is, it was humiliating for her when the police got involved. Since Janine's family didn't press charges, the police weren't too harsh, but there had to be legal repercussions. Paul was sentenced to community service – cleaning around the village, like litter-picking and removing graffiti. Shaken, he accepted his fate; Ma felt that it would have been inappropriate for him to be able to escape all consequences, but it made her feel even more ashamed of what had happened. Now, she isn't as upset, but Paul is still as distraught as ever. Ma tried to hug him this morning and, to her surprise, was shakily rejected by a trembling Paul, pallid and mumbling something about not deserving it. Ma's anger didn't last, it kind of fizzled away like mine did eventually, but Pa was sterner. He still stops Paul and eyes him gravely and sits him down for a serious lecture. I don't know what they talk about. I've asked Paul, but he doesn't want to tell me. Paul comes out of these talks with Pa meek and often bleary-eyed, looking extremely exhausted, even though all he did was listen to Pa. Maybe they're to do with his drinking – if so, they've helped, because as far as I know, he hasn't touched alcohol since the accident. He looks as sickly as ever, but he's sober. I suppose the accident did have a sort of positive effect on Paul.

I stumbled upon the car again, months after Paul had stowed it away into a far corner of the garage. It wasn't as shiny as I remembered; I thought that Paul had stored it here to continue caring for it, but it looked totally forgotten – covered in dust and cobwebs. It didn't matter. I still wanted to take a nail and scratch at the red paint. I thought that Paul was still using it, but hiding it away because he was too sentimental to get rid of it? That was worse. I was just furious with him. It was like he didn't even care. Soon, though, the anger dissipated and I was left in a much stranger state – I was so worried, all the time. I kept thinking about the accident, imagining what it must have felt like for Janine as the car crashed. I could imagine her ma screaming or crying or something, and Paul panicked and frenzied and guilty. I could never picture Janine's reaction though; or maybe I didn't want to. I definitely didn't want to think too much about the physical pain she was in. Anyway, I don't know how other people react when one of their best friends is in a car crash, but me and Winnie and Bea have been kind of miserable ever since. It's horrible. I wish it hadn't happened.

6

Bea

Gran has been getting progressively worse. I don't know what to do. I'm consumed with thoughts of Janine too; I can't do anything, but I wish I could do everything to help her. We haven't even seen her yet, because Gina says she isn't ready. Cameron asks her every time, almost pleading her, but she doesn't relent. I want to see Janine too, obviously, but part of me is scared that it's worse than we think; that she's not the same. If she isn't, then I wouldn't know how to react.

But Gran health is deteriorating more and more, and I feel so helpless because nothing I am doing is helping.

7

Janine

It's lunch time. Nurse Adams waddles into the room, pushing a creaking trolley with hot food wobbling on it.

"I'm hungry," a moody teenage girl opposite me in the room grumbles. Mum, sitting by my side, rolls her eyes and pats my hand.

"Yes, doll," the nurse replies absent-mindedly. "Just a moment…"

Suddenly, the teenage swears loudly, earning a stunned, wide-eyed look from Nurse Adams. Everyone else in the room is pretty shocked too – all the other little girls stare delightedly at the drama… all except for sweet little Betty, who hasn't actually realised what is going on, and is happily playing pat-a-cake by herself.

To be honest, I'm not very surprised. I've seen a lot of this girl lately (I think her name is Tabby) and I've come to know that she often gets very fed up with everyone and starts insulting them. Well. That's not strictly true. I've heard her mumbling to herself at night, listing off all her enemies, having heart-felt conversations with herself, thinking there no one else was awake. It's quite sad, really. If I weren't so scared of her, I would've quite liked to be friends.

Nurse Adams stares at her for a few solid moments; Tabby stares defiantly back. I wonder briefly if that's how it's all going to turn out with me. It's a very strange thought. Will I still be as stubborn and short-tempered in the future as I am now? I glance down at my legs and in a heartbeat, I've realised. Yeah. That's how it's going to be.

A few more silent seconds tick by. Betty laughs quietly by herself in the corner.

From next to me, Mum hisses in a cold, hushed, slightly exhausted tone, "What a mess."

I look at her, mildly surprised. Mum's expression is hard-set and she's watching Tabby. Nurse Adams is also looking at Tabby accusingly, but after a few moments, her expression softens and she goes to her, taking her creaking trolley with her.

"Are you OK, darling?" I hear her murmur. Tabby nods immediately and then everyone looks away hurriedly.

"Humph!" Mum says loudly. "How rude!"

I roll my eyes at her. "Mum, come on. You'd get pretty fed up once in a while too." Mum frowns sympathetically and squeezes my hand.

"Are you lonely, darling?" she asks gently. It seems like a sort of random question – after a few moments of consideration, I say,

"Er... I don't know. What do you mean?" But Mum ignores me, lost in her thoughts. Her blue eyes are hazy.

A few seconds later, I think out loud, "What should I get for lunch today?"

Mum leaves the question hanging. I glance at her.

"Mum?"

Again, no answer.

"Mum!"

She turns to me finally. "Sweetheart, I'll be right back, just hold on for a few minutes, alright?"

I stare at her, frowning slightly.

"OK..."

She smiles and nods at me, and rushes out the door, abandoning another cold cup of tea on my bedside table. So abruptly, she is gone.

A lot longer than a few minutes go by before Mum comes back. We – the other girls in the ward and I – have had lunch, and a nice long chat with Nurse Adams too, so by the time Mum comes back, it's almost four.

"Hi M–"I start, but stop on my tracks. Has my mouth stopped working?

In the doorway behind Mum stand Winnie, Cameron and Bea. Winnie is the first to come inside – she looks around with wide, perceptive eyes and drinks in the whole scene. A small smile plays on her lips as she turns back around to glance at Cameron, her skirt rustling. That's when I notice: her skirt is plain black and knee-length. She's wearing long socks and a crisp white shirt. She holds a gorilla-sized black blazer in one hand – somehow, I have a feeling she looks good in it anyway. I gulp hard.

Bea grins and looks at me straight away; the simple honesty in her eyes makes me wince. I see her look at my legs on the bed once, twice, before staring for a few long seconds. My heart pounds in my chest like a caged animal. It feels like it'll jump out my mouth. Bea's wearing exactly the same as Winnie, only her shirt is not quite as brightly white, and the leather on her shoes is a little torn.

Cameron comes in last. His face is expressionless. His blazer seems to reach up to his knees; his shoes look too big; his shirt is dishevelled and falls out of his trousers. His blue eyes seem fixated in a faraway point. He isn't smiling.

"Look, Janine, your friends have come to visit!" Mum says, breaking the silence. The grin on her face stretches her rouged mouth unnaturally. I can't will myself to smile back at her.

I hear the clacking of Winnie's shoes on the floor as she walks slowly towards me.

"...Hi," she says, smiling. Hers is a real smile.

I lick my dry lips and gulp again.

Bea approaches my bed too now. Her beam reaches up to her ears, as usual, but I don't have it in me to smile back.

"How have you been?!" she exclaims, so loudly that some of the other girls in the ward that hadn't already been watching now turn to look curiously. I feel my cheeks getting hot.

"We've missed you," Bea continues, patting my hand sympathetically.

"We've missed you so much, Janine," Winnie adds.

I've missed them too. Tears prick my eyes, and I blink them away quickly.

I stare at them for a few moments. How bizarre – they're in school uniform. They've started school. They've started secondary school without me.

Cameron still hasn't said a word. His face is sickly yellow. I don't think he's even looked at me since he walked in. Winnie sees me staring at him and looks too.

"Cam?" she whispers to him. "Are you feeling alright?"

I bite down a flash of annoyance. Since when does she call him 'Cam'?

He doesn't reply. It worries me, and I can tell it worries Mum too.

"Cameron, darling, do you want to step outside for a breath of fresh air?" she asks him gently. He shakes his head, and lifts his gaze slowly from the floor to my hospital bed; the wall behind me; my hands. He's looking anywhere but at my legs or at me.

"How- how have you been doing?" he says finally. It sounds almost scripted, like he prepared it. I gulp nervously – and then I gulp again, and again, trying to swallow back the lump in my throat. It seems to get bigger and bigger until it surfaces, and I feel my face contort, and it all comes out as a massive sob. It's an animalistic sound; a sound that racks my body. At first, I don't even notice Mum's arms around me. I don't even notice her take Winnie and Bea and Cameron away. I don't even notice the rest of the world. All I know is that I can't walk, or run, or skip or jump or sprint, and I can't keep up with my friends. Although they probably don't even want to be my friends anymore.

※◆※

8

Cameron

We catch a glimpse of Janine when she's let out of the hospital – me and Winnie and Bea – as we're walking home from school. She's sitting there, shivering, staring ahead defiantly with tear marks on her cheeks. Her ma is pushing her wheelchair calmly. Neither of them spots us as they head towards their house. No one speaks. Winnie shuts her mouth for once and stands there, eyes gaping wide, rooted to the spot. Bea is frozen too, although she'd never normally pass up on a chance to say hello. She looks sad, which is an emotion rarely seen on Bea's face. Her smiling cheeks droop.

It's strange, but I don't really feel anything. My feet are anchored to the ground. I can't move. Janine looks so different. She's even thinner; her grey eyes stick out of her face bulbously. I'm almost scared of her. Is she still our friend? It doesn't look like she wants to be. I can't see her laughing and screaming with Winnie like she did a few months ago in the summer. That's all been blown out like a candle by bitter gusts of wind and battering October rain. The thought of Janine never being able to walk again hits me like a punch to the stomach, and I can judge, looking from Winnie's grim face, that she feels the same. Only Bea has resumed her happy, carefree state.

"Come on, you guys!" she says, skipping a few paces ahead of us. I glance at Winnie, who now looks slightly nauseous, wondering if I should do something to comfort her.

"I should get home," she says, her voice a little louder than a whisper. I nod quickly.

"Can you come out tomorrow?" I ask. Tomorrow is a Saturday, and normally, we all meet up whenever we can.

"Sure," she says, forcing a quick smile. Her parents really aren't as bad as she makes out; I met them once, and they seemed lovely. They let Winnie out all the time now, as long as she's back before it gets dark and she does her chores, and she says they were really sympathetic about Janine and even brought in a big pink bouquet of flowers for her one morning.

"What time?" Bea butts in. Winnie shrugs half-heartedly.

"I don't know, eleven maybe? I have some housework to do,"

I nod. "Alright,"

We all stand there in silence, not sure what else to say.

"Right." I say slowly. "I have to go,"

"Yes, me too," Winnie jumps in. She waves, smiles and walks off quickly. I turn to Bea and smile awkwardly.

"Bye," I say. She yells "bye" back and I walk home, thinking of Janine.

9

Bea

I was with Cameron and Winnie when we saw Janine after she was let out of the hospital. We'd just gotten out of school, and it was cold and windy and I didn't have a coat and I wanted to go home. When I saw Janine, I thought about waving and grinning, because then she might have smiled back, but I didn't. She didn't look like how she was before. She looked more grown-up and serious. I felt a pang of sadness. A long time had passed. What if she wasn't the same anymore? What if Winnie was right, and this was all my fault for leaving the house at the summer festival? The guilt was surging in me. I felt like bursting into tears. This was all my fault, and Janine was never getting better. And Gran is getting sicker still. I'm ruining everything. Sometimes I feel like asking Gran about the witch rumours, but how can I?

10

Janine

The Saturday after I'm let out of hospital, at ten in the morning, there's a hesitant knock at the door.

"Who the bloody–" Mum mutters angrily, waking up with a start and stumbling off the sofa we'd slept on. I struggle to sit up, blinking at the dusty light spilling through our windows. I hear Mum open the front door and I stop moving, trying to hear what's happening; I imagine my ears twitching like a rabbit's. The door unlocks and squeaks open.

"Good morning," I hear a male voice.

"Wh–" Mum exclaims.

"I'm sorry, I heard that Janine was back, and I..."

"...You what?" Mum retorts.

The person clears his voice anxiously. "I... I don't know."

Mum scoffs. "It's a bit late for this, you know,"

"I'm sorry." he says quietly. I hear Mum sigh.

"Let's talk later," she says more gently. "Give us half an hour, we'll meet you–"

"Come to our house, Ma's so eager to see Janine too," he pauses. "Please."

"Alright. We'll be there. Half an hour."

The door shuts.

"Mum!" I call impatiently.

"Come on darling, let's get you dressed." Mum says, coming into the room. She looks more tired than she did before we went to sleep.

"Who was that?" I demand. Rather than telling me off for being rude, I catch Mum stifling a smile.

"What?"

"You haven't really changed at all, have you?"

I smile as well.

"Thank God," she says, helping me into my wheelchair.

"Who was at the door, please? Why were they asking about me?"

Mum is firmer now. "You'll see. We're meeting him soon."

"Why won't you just tell me?" I protest.

"Because if I do, you won't come."

I should have seen it coming. Honestly. I don't know how I didn't guess it would be him.

Mum wheeled me out of the house, past our little street, through the market – with steely patience to the staring townspeople – and up towards the puny hill. The hill leading to the farmhouse.

"Mum?" I call uncertainly as she pushes me, earth getting caught in the wheels. "Mum?"

"Yes, Janine?" Mum sounds strangely calm.

"Mum, why are we here?" My voice comes out a lot more hysterical than I had intended.

"We're meeting with–"

"With who?"

We come to the top of the hill. The door to the farmhouse is ajar, and he is just outside.

"Hi, Janine." Paul says.

No. No. I can't do this.

I stare at him, blinking slowly. "Mum, no." I mutter. I'm certain that she hears me, but she doesn't react and instead steps towards him, smiling.

"How are you? How has your family been? Is your mum alright?" she says politely. Paul nods awkwardly and smiles back.

"Ma's just inside, she's, erm, she's really excited to see you guys."

We go inside. I stare at Paul's back. He's wearing just a t-shirt. Isn't he cold?

His mum is in the hallway, waiting for us. She's exactly as I remember her: tidy, plump and rosy-cheeked.

"Oh, Janine, you poor dear!" she instantly exclaims. I see Mum's annoyed expression.

"She's been getting a lot better," she says.

"Yeah, you look great, Janine," Paul says, smiling kindly. I gulp. I don't look great, I look terrible. I've been through so much pain, and it's not even over yet, I still can't walk, and it's all his fault. He was driving; he crashed. He caused this. He put me in a wheelchair.

I don't reply, and I glance at him quickly. He looks a little hurt now, and I can't help but feel a bit guilty.

"Let's all have a nice little catch-up, then," Mum says quietly after a few seconds of grim silence.

"How lovely," Paul's mum murmurs.

Mum glares at me.

"Mhm," I quickly agree.

"So," Mum begins. "What have you been up to lately, Paul?"

He shrugs, his face reddening like I remember Cameron's used to. "Nothing much."

"Oh," his mum clucks fondly. "He's so modest. He's working at getting his driving license, my smart boy... and he helps his Pa so much on the farm nowadays... very hardworking, you know... such a good big brother to little Cam, he teaches him so much, helps him with his chores and his homework... really, he's a wonder..."

"Ma?" there's a voice behind me.

Adrenaline rushes in my body; I swivel my wheelchair around to face him so fast that when I look back at Mum, I see her sitting in trance-like shock and pride.

He stands there, in a baggy, scruffy old t-shirt that was probably handed down to him from Paul, his muddy boots still on, his eyes striking and blue, his hair the same soft, glowing halo of blond I remember it to be.

"Hi, Cameron," Mum says cheerily.

"Hello, how are you?" he replies in a monotone, his face blank.

"Ah, we've been doing alright," Mum says, smiling around the room. Paul nods slowly and grins back awkwardly. His mum's cheeks go even redder than usual.

"Such a horrid affair, I... no amount of apologies will ever express our sympathy, Janine." she murmurs under her breath, standing up, smiling at me sympathetically and patting my hand like I'm a small, run-down puppy. "Just a minute, my dears, I need to go and feed the hens."

She waddles out, leaving the rest of us in silence.

"So..." Paul starts, pulling up a chair next to my wheelchair. "What have you been doing lately?"

I don't reply. I see Cameron still standing gawkily by the door.

Mum nudges me sharply. "I'm great, yeah, thanks," I immediately blurt out.

Cameron slowly sits down in an armchair opposite us. "How was it?" he asks, showing the tiniest bit of emotion for the first time – a frown knit over his eyebrows.

I swallow uneasily. "How was what?"

"The hospital."

I think back. I think of the needles and the nurses and the creaky hospital beds and the blissfully happy little girls (like Betty) and the stubbornly *un*happy girls (like me; like Tabby). I think of the frustration of not being able to walk; the struggle of the physiotherapy; the doubts; the disappointment; the determination. I think of Mum, snoring gently in the chair beside my bed, and seeing Winnie and Cameron and Bea again. It was difficult.

"It wasn't too bad," I reply instead.

"Hmm," Cameron nods, seeming reassured.

Just then, Cameron and Paul's mum calls from the kitchen. "Gina, love? You want a cuppa?"

Mum squeezes my hand and stands up. "I think I'll leave you kids to talk, then," she says, almost skipping out the room.

There are a few seconds of silence.

"We really missed you, Janine," Paul says, looking me directly in the eyes. It makes me twitch uncomfortably. He laughs quietly. "I can tell *you* haven't missed *me* very much. It's fine. I get it. I'll go away if you want. Do you want me to go?"

I stare at him. "I don't want you to go away."

He breathes a sigh of relief and offers one of his lopsided grins. I catch Cameron observing us thoughtfully.

"I want to go," I say impulsively. I didn't even know I was going to say it until I heard the words come out my mouth.

"You want to go home?" Paul asks, looking concerned.

I consider this. "No." I reply decidedly.

"Um, outside? You want some fresh air? It is a bit stuffy in here…" Paul says, scratching the back of his neck.

I think about this. I don't know. I don't know why I said anything in the first place. I know where I want to go, and it's impossible anyway – I want to go back to the summer, before any of this happened. I've gone over it a thousand times in my head. This didn't have to happen.

And yet it did.

"Yes, please," I say instead.

"Hey," Cameron says suddenly. "Do you want to see Dolly?"

I instantly perk up. Dolly, Dolly the cow! I'd almost forgotten all about her, and yet, now that I think of it, I've actually missed her terribly.

"She's out on the field, Cam," Paul murmurs.

"It's not that far," he argues.

"She's in a *wheelchair*, Cameron!" Paul bellows. I wince, and he sees it. "Oh no, sorry, I didn't mean it like that, I'm sure we'll find a way–"

"No thank you, that's alright," I reply coolly. "I think I've changed my mind, sorry."

I look at Paul, *really* look at him now. His face is pale and sweaty; his hands paper-white, with bulging veins etched on. There's a dark wet patch on the back of his t-shirt, even though it's the middle of October. He keeps fiddling with a loose string hanging from his top.

"Sorry, Janine," he says truthfully. "I'm a complete mess. Sorry."

I glance at Cameron. He's staring at Paul with his kind, sympathetic eyes. I gulp.

I close my eyes and see Paul grinning confidently in the driver's seat, the way the smile dipped in his cheeks. I see Mum smiling back. I see the wind ruffling my hair.

The car swerves. It's all happening in slow motion. The car door opens. I feel myself falling out, slowly, horribly slowly. I feel the impact of the cold, hard ground. Forever passes by, and I'm still lying on the floor, sobbing. I can't move my legs.

I open my eyes and look down. I can't move my legs.

"It's alright, Paul." I say, my voice croaky and rough. It's not alright.

It starts to rain as Mum wheels me back. Hard, heavy raindrops, not light drizzle. I don't say a thing the whole journey, and neither does Mum. By the time we get back home, we're soaked to the skin.

11

Winnie

I wake up to hear Mother and Father laughing together in the kitchen. The sweet, doughy smell of pancakes wafts in the air. I stumble downstairs, still half asleep, stomping with each step; yet, when I walk into the kitchen Mother and Father are staring, smiling, entranced, at each other, completely unaware that I'm even there.

"Good morning," I say, eyeing the stack of golden-brown pancakes next to them.

"Hello, my Winnie," Mother says warmly, putting an arm around me. I grin.

"Winifred." Father quips, smiling with a fuzzy sort of kindness.

"Father." I reply, a little confused.

"We have some wonderful news," he continues. Mother beams next to him. I stare at them, a little bit stunned.

"I don't understand..."

Father sighs. "Winnie, a few months ago, your mother was... expecting, shall we say."

I am completely, utterly lost.

"However, there were some... complications." Father resumes. "That is all in the past. That news was rather morbid, Win, I know, but we have some very exciting news now. Your mother is now expecting again!"

I look from one to the other. Mother looks so sunny and warm; Father looks as though he could burst from the excitement. I still have no idea what they are talking about.

"What is she expecting?" I ask.

Mother glances at Father and smiles. "A child, Winifred. I'm expecting a child. I'm pregnant, my dear." She pats a tender hand over mine.

"A child? A... a baby?" It clicks, just then. That's what all those doctor trips were about. That's why Mother was so upset. It all feels like a lifetime ago.

"Yes," Father laughs. "A little brother or sister for you."

Mother rubs her stomach fondly, smiling down at it as though it were already a real baby.

"Isn't it amazing?" she murmurs.

I smile and nod, but I'm not sure if she was talking to me, to herself or to the baby.

12

Cameron

Seeing Janine at the farm this morning was so much worse than I expected it to be. I could see on her face that she didn't want to be there. If only Paul hadn't crashed his car... if only Paul wouldn't have turned everything upside down. I miss her so much. When I saw her sitting sensibly, there, all big eyes and puffy hair and blotchy skin, I suddenly knew, like it clicked. Any remaining hope ebbed out of me. There's nothing to do anymore.

The sun is setting over the yellowing hills as I help Ma pack up her things at her jewellery stall when a familiar figure approaches us. As she gets closer, I recognise Janine's ma, trekking towards us from her own clothes stall, a fixed smile on her face.

"Gina!" Ma exclaims cheerily when she's close enough. "You alright, love?"

"Yes, I'm fine," she smiles. "Just been packing up,"

"Yeah, me too, Cam's just helping me," Ma says, patting my shoulder. I look up at Janine's ma with the brightest smile I can muster.

"I actually came over to speak to Cameron as well," she says thoughtfully. Oh no. What did I do?

"It's... I just wanted to ask if you'd like to come to our house for a few hours... you know, you and the two girls... to play, to play amongst yourselves." She stutters anxiously. "Would that be alright?"

"Oh, I think that'd be lovely!" Ma says happily. "Don't you think, Cam? How nice of you to invite him, thank you,"

They natter on for ages, and I only start paying attention when it becomes evident that they're making plans for something.

"We can't today, of course–" Ma starts.

"Yes, it is getting quite dark; I dare say you'll want to have your tea soon–"

"And tomorrow's Sunday, we couldn't possibly; we have church on Sundays–"

"I understand, of course... how about after school on Monday?"

Ma nods, satisfied, and waves her goodbye. "Let's go, Cam." She says, yanking my arm.

13

Janine

The day after we go to see Paul and Cameron at the farm is a wet, grey Sunday. Mum wakes me up with a big smile on her face that I can't bring myself to return and she says,

"Janine, I have an idea."

Uh-oh. "What's that, Mum?"

"Well." She starts delightedly. "I thought we might go to church today. You know, seeing as there's one in the village and all."

Whatever it was I expected her to say, it certainly wasn't that. "But Mum..." I say, my voice still a little raspy from sleeping. "There's always been a church in the village. We've never really gone to church. Why start–"

"Why start now?" she finishes for me. "Because... because, why not? We might as well make the most of the day while it's nice and early. Look, sweetie, it's a lovely morning," she gazes out the window, smiling dreamily.

I follow her eyes. It's soggy and muddy and windy outside.

"Mum," I begin slowly. "Is.... Is there some bloke that you've met at the church or something?"

Mum spins around back to face me. "Yes, actually." She says earnestly.

My face freezes.

Mum laughs. "The *priest*, Janine. I talked to some of the people at the church when you were in the hospital, and they insisted on mentioning you in today's prayers." She nibbles her lip nervously.

126

I almost sigh with relief. But then I process what she's just said, and my feelings change immediately.

"Mum, I'm not *dead*."

"I know, Janine, don't be silly. I just thought…"

I stare at her. "Could God make my legs better?"

"I don't know," Mum replies, putting a hand on my shoulder. "Let's see."

I should have thought this through. It's too late to turn back now. Mum and I are standing in the doorway leading into the church. Everyone inside is staring blankly at us, and we're staring back with similar expressions at them.

"Ah, hello Gina," an old man dressed in robes says, approaching Mum. He has very little hair, sparse and snowy-white, and it grows around the edges of his temples. His hands are plump and pink, and spidery white hairs sprout from the knuckles.

"And… Janine. I've heard quite bit about you, my dear." He says, his voice deep and resounding, like the bottom of a well. He takes one of my hands in his, which now looks peculiarly bony and small and cold in comparison. I look at him carefully, at his wrinkles and his big, warm hands and his potbelly sticking out through his robes.

"The ceremony shall start soon," he says, his voice more hushed. Offering us one last kind smile, he walks away, all calm and serene, leaving Mum and I dithering awkwardly.

I keep glancing at Mum every couple of seconds, expecting her to burst out laughing. We're sitting stiffly on slippery wooden benches inside an icy hall – well, she sits on the bench and I'm in my wheelchair at the end of the bench next to her. We watch as the other people file inside, filling up each row, talking to each other quickly but very quietly. Mum stares ahead, deadly serious, her back straight against the cold bench, waiting. I'm not quite sure what we're waiting for, to be honest. But finally, the priest shows up at the front, looking very grand and regal in his swishing robes. I look around the hall, taking in all the people. I had no idea there were so many people that came here. My heart freezes. There's Cameron. I can see him, huddled away, squashed in a corner next to his mum.

I look away quickly. I'm not sure why, but I don't really want him to see me.

"Janine, if you would please wave at everyone, dear, so we can all see where you are?" I hear the priest's booming voice.

I spin around to look at Mum.

"What's he on about?" I whisper. Mum scowls, annoyed, and I wave around uncertainly. Everyone smiles sympathetically at me, some already murmuring prayers under their breaths. It all makes me very nervous.

"He was telling everyone all about you," Mum hisses in my ear. "Why on Earth weren't you listening?"

"Sorry," I say distractedly, glancing at Cameron. He was just looking at me. He must have been. I saw his gaze flick away just in time.

"It's fine." Mum sighs. "Pay attention. We're here for you, remember."

Cameron's just staring at his shoes now, rather dismally. Did I upset him? That's the last thing I want to do. Being friends with him and Winnie and Bea has been a little different since the accident, and it's scary to think that we might be getting more and more distanced.

My eyes snap back into focus. What's that smell?

I try to see what the priest is doing at the front. He seems to be waving around something filled with incense.

I glance at Mum. Her nose is all funny and wrinkled up. I don't think she's enjoying this as much as she thought she would.

The priest motions to everyone and a woman from behind him pops up and sits down at the organ. A few people stand up. Mum and I don't. Before I have time to digest this, the woman plays a resounding chord on the organ and everyone starts singing a hymn. I've heard it before I think, but I don't sing along, even though there's a sheet on the bench with the words to it. I hear Mum singing along under her breath.

I remain very puzzled by everything that's going on for the entirety of the ceremony, and whenever I try to ask Mum what's happening she hushes me hurriedly, telling me to be quiet and pay attention. Well, that doesn't help at all. I entertain myself watching the burning candles near the front of the hall, my eyes following the flickering flames, lined up together and moving almost in unison. I notice Mum looking at me, tight-lipped and irritated that I'm not paying attention properly, and I drag my gaze away from the mesmerising fire. I look up and around hopefully, desperate to go home at last, but the priest seems to now be reciting some sort of Bible story, and it's all taking ages. Glancing around the hall, everyone else looks entranced and completely gripped – even Mum is taking an interest, her eyes burning into the priest – except me. Except me... and Cameron. He's staring blankly at a stained glass window in front of him. I wonder how many times he's had to stare at that. He looks bored.

Suddenly, and seemingly without any cause, he drags his gaze away from it and turns slowly around to look at me. I gulp. It feels like my face has frozen stiff. We're both uncomfortably expressionless and I don't know what to do. I want to smile and wave and go over and talk to him, but I don't.

⚜

14

Cameron

I had no idea Janine and her ma would be at church. They've never been before.

I kind of want to talk to her. I know I can't in the middle of the church hall, but something hasn't been sitting right with me since she came to our house and talked to Paul. Call me crazy, but I wish we could've gone to see Dolly in the field. Maybe we could've caught up a little and made things less awkward.

I wonder if she can see how miserable I am. I hope not. Should I smile, show that I'm alright? She looks so scary, with those hard grey eyes; those jutting cheekbones; that pulled-back hair. I don't really remember being *intimidated* of her before. Was she always like this? Maybe she was. Maybe she just wasn't with me.

I'm going to smile. How badly could it go? Smiling is my go-to action when things are awkward.

I do it. I smile. She can probably tell it's fake.

For a moment, I wonder, horrified, if she really isn't going to smile back.

Then...

She smiles, looking so relieved. It softens all her features – it makes her look so warm and kind.

"Cam, for goodness sake!" Ma screeches. I look around. Everyone is getting up. I hadn't even noticed. She pulls my arm and yanks me to my feet.

"Thank you," she nods seriously at the priest. He smiles and waves at both of us. I don't wave back. I'm not quite sure why he seems to think we're friends. I mean, he's, like, ninety-six.

Paul's friends were all older than him, but not by whole entire centuries, like the priest. They all had about a million girlfriends all over the place and liked to stay up late and drink a lot. For a while, Paul continued to go to the city, but I think he found that it lost its charm without the drinking. He has completely stopped drinking, and now he's stopped going up to the city too.

"Cam, get a move on," she says, ushering me out the door. Outside, the sky is still as dismal and grey as it was earlier this morning, and it doesn't cheer me up very much.

I linger a little outside the church, wondering if I should wait for Janine to try and talk to her.

"Cameron!" Ma calls crossly, placing a podgy hand on my shoulder and guiding me carefully away. "Silly boy, you're seeing her tomorrow after school anyway, aren't you?"

Suddenly, I'm not so sure I want to talk to her.

15

Winnie

Cameron passes me a note during our tedious physics lesson today. The paper is a messy sheet torn out from his exercise book, all greyish and lined. He'd folded it up 4 times, in a rush because the corners don't meet up with each other. I stifle excitement, thinking that he was admitting some sorts of feelings for me, but the note doesn't at all say what I expect it to.

janines ma invited us over to their house after school. you wanna come?

I tut at his bad grammar, trying hard to not to look offended. He only talks about Janine nowadays. I'd never admit it, but I'm getting a bit sick of all this.

I catch his eye and nod quickly. He smiles his dimpled smile, his eyes crinkling at the corners, looking relieved, and it feels like melting butter, like warm grass, like sweet, battered apples from a meadow. And I can't help but smile back and wonder why I was ever annoyed in the first place.

"Hello, Winnie," Mother beams as I come in. Her hands cup around an invisible baby bump, like she's keeping it safe. Father sits at the kitchen table, messing with the wires in a lightbulb. I have no idea what he's doing, but it looks very professional.

"Hi, Mother, Father," I say.

I ask them about going to Janine's house, and they agree readily, even though it's a weekday, which I don't think would've been the case if Janine had a pair of healthy, working legs.

A little while later, I'm hurriedly dressed out of my school uniform and I wait outside my house for Cameron to turn up, because even though Janine's house is a few metres away, I don't want to go in by myself. A few minutes later, Cameron comes walking around the corner, Bea dawdling behind. She has something enclosed in her pink fist.

"Look, Winnie!" she exclaims. She unfolds her fingers and I see a sweaty pebble trapped inside.

"Very pretty," I say nervously. I haven't really spoken to Bea in a long time, even though we go to the same school and are in the same classes. It makes me feel a little bit guilty sometimes that she's all alone in class.

Together, we all take a deep breath and walk up to Janine's front door.

My heart pounds.

16

Cameron

I was kind of relying on Winnie to be loud and aloof like she normally is, but if anything, she seems more nervous than *me*.

I'm the one that knocks. Winnie just hangs back awkwardly, and Bea is distracted by a chip in one of the bricks that build up the porch.

I clear my throat. It sounds too loud and obvious.

The door bursts open, and Janine's ma stands there, grinning at us with the energy of an excitable puppy.

"Come in, come in!" she says. She gives us all cups of orange juice, and I start to feel myself relax a bit.

"Janine will be out in just a moment," she says, and she rushes away to a different room to help Janine get dressed or something.

My stomach twists again. I look at Winnie and Bea. They're sitting in armchairs opposite each other, staring blankly. Bea is idly kicking at Winnie's chair, and Winnie is staring blankly at her.

"Were your parents alright about coming over here?" I ask her, feeling that I have to say something. Winnie looks up at me, surprised, and nods.

"They were–"

The door opens then, and Janine comes in, her wheelchair pushed by her ma (who's still beaming crazily).

"They were fine." Winnie whispers to finish, not looking at me.

"Hi Janine!" Bea exclaims, for once thinking quicker than us.

"Hello Janine," Winnie says hurriedly.

"Hi," I parrot stupidly.

Janine exhales. I wonder if she's got any idea how nervous we all are. "Hi."

17

Bea

I asked Gran before I left the house this time. I got a weary nod of a response before she drifted back to sleep. I was restless, though, and wouldn't stop fretting over her: I carefully tucked her in her thin, flimsy blanket; I made her a fresh cup of tea and placed it on her bedside table; I even left her a book in case she woke up and got bored, though I knew deep inside that she wouldn't feel strong enough to read it. I almost didn't want to go, even though I really wanted to see Janine and Cameron and Winnie. I was anxious that something would happen to Gran if I left her alone. But Janine's beautiful house was calling, so I slipped into my school shoes and left the house.

When I meet up with my friends outside Janine's house, they both seem a bit on edge. I start up a game of observing the nature around me, in my head. I count four pretty golden leaves on the ground, and more than a dozen crushed dead ones. I find a shiny pebble too, which I take with me and squeeze in my palm.

"Look, Winnie!" I say, and she smiles at me uncertainly and it makes me feel delighted that she isn't being mean anymore. Then the front door opens and it's Janine's ma, standing there cheerily, her eyes smiling at us like little blue stars. She takes us into a living room, which is exciting at first because it looks fabulous and classy, but Janine isn't there so it quickly turns a bit boring. I'm about to ask Cameron where Janine is when she comes in, sitting in her wheelchair, with her soft hair down on her shoulders and her eyes big and nervous.

"Hi Janine!" I call out. Janine looks at me and beams, and I beam back, and it's like sunshine in a room because we're both so smiley. I suddenly realise how much I've missed her.

⋯⋯◄❀►⋯⋯

18

Janine

Sometimes, I think that Mum is more invested in my friendships than I am. She went out specially to buy juice and snacks for us and everything. It makes me feel bad for not wanting to do anything all day, but not bad enough to get up and get something done.

It came as a pleasant surprise to me when Mum didn't insist I wear some ridiculous, sparkle-adorned dress. I think she knew how nervous I'd be about it, and she let me wear my floppy, comfortable jeans. They're actually a bit short and only come up to where my ankles begin, but Mum didn't notice so it's fine. I'd mostly just worn loose, comfy clothing like sweaters and tracksuit bottoms after my accident, and a lot of my other clothes had gotten small on me. It's puzzling, because I still look as scrawny as ever, but Mum's always saying how I'm so big and understanding now, so maybe I *have* grown.

My friends have grown a lot too. I hadn't really noticed it before, but now that we're all packed in our living room, I'm seeing all sorts of things. Winnie's twisty, black hair has been pulled into tight, shiny braids on her head. It looks really nice, and makes me blush when I think of my own unkempt hair. Cameron's hair is all messy like mine, but it looks fluffy and adorable, like a golden little baby chick. He jitters nervously, shifting from foot to foot, and it makes me smile because it's like he hasn't changed it all. He sees this, and maybe he takes it the wrong way because his cheeks go rosy pink. Bea is as dreamy as she has always been too. I see her look curiously around the room; she grins when her eyes come to rest on me.

"You look really pretty, Janine," she says kindly. A smile seeps through my cheeks.

"Thanks. You look nice too." I quickly observe her, and decide that that isn't really very true. She hasn't changed out of her school uniform fully – she's still wearing her grubby grey shirt, which isn't completely tucked into her skirt. Her knee-high socks have green grass stains on them. It's freezing outside, I don't know how she isn't cold. I ignore this though, and add hurriedly for Cameron and Winnie, "You…you guys too."

Mum is taking Bea in too. "Bea, do you want to borrow a jacket or a cardigan or something from me? Aren't you cold?"

Bea shakes her head without even considering it. "Oh, I couldn't. Thanks though." She looks away and takes a loud slurp from her cup of juice.

Mum raises her eyebrows, then nods reluctantly. "Alright… hey, Winnie, I heard your mum's having a baby, congratulations!"

"Yes, um, thank you," Winnie replies, stroking the red velvet of her armchair with her thumb. There's a long silence. Mum sighs.

"I suppose there's lots of catching up to do, hmm? I'll leave you all to it," she shuffles towards the door, but pauses before exiting. "Shout if you need anything. Have fun."

"Thanks Mum," I say, shooting her a smile. Then she leaves, and we're all silent.

"Soooo," Winnie starts, dragging the word out. "How have you been, Janine?"

"Fine." I tell her. I realise a few seconds too late that that sounds a bit rude, and I try to make amends. "I –"

"Can you walk again yet?" Bea interrupts. She stares at me with doe eyes, completely unaware of how direct of a question that is.

Winnie, opposite her on her armchair, stamps on her foot furiously. "*Bea!*"

"What?" she blinks obliviously. "Can you, Janine? I can teach you if you like." She stands up and takes a few steps forward towards me. "See, it's easy!"

"No." I say slowly, trying to keep it together. "I can't... just yet. Maybe I'll be able to one day."

"How about today?" Bea replies. Winnie stamps on her foot again, refusing to look me in the eye. Cameron is beetroot-red.

"Maybe not today, Bea." I tell her. She doesn't say anything. "Hey, it's alright. Let's talk about something else," I attempt to remedy the situation. "Do you want to go out?" Winnie suggests. I shudder at the thought of all the townspeople ogling at me as I wheel myself through the village.

"No thanks."

"We could go out to my house," Cameron chips in, speaking properly for the first time since they'd arrived. "You could see Dolly."

I almost say yes, before remembering that Paul will inevitably be there. "I wish, but we can't. Sorry." He smiles nervously, seeming pleased that I'd talked to him.

"Let's just stay in." I say.

"And play!" Bea exclaims.

"And *talk*." Winnie corrects her.

And so we do.

I'd forgotten how much of a gossip Winnie is. Once she gets started, she keeps talking on and on, sharing funny little details and quirks about just about everyone in the village. She tells me about school – all the children, all the teachers. At first it makes me feel a bit like I'm on the outside of all this, but she has such a way of entertaining everyone that I soon forget all that and laugh along with everyone else. Well... Bea often misunderstands the jokes and her attention drifts away from the conversation, and Cameron isn't at all happy with talking about people behind their backs and refuses to join in, but Winnie and I have such a good time that I don't even mind.

"Hi kids," Mum says, poking her head around the door suddenly. "Do you need anything? I don't mind getting you some juice, or snacks,"

"Could I have some juice please?" Winnie asks politely. Mum nods, delighted to help. She comes back a minute later, gives me a quick smile lingers by the door.

"What do you want to play?" Bea suddenly bursts out while Winnie sips her juice.

"I don't know," I reply vaguely.

"I could bring out your old plush toys if you like, Janine," Mum suggests. My face flushes and I shake my head.

"I could..." she starts, looking around at each of our faces. "Leave you alone?"

I nod quickly and apologetically, but Mum seems quite happy to leave at last. "Like I said, I'll be... I'll be in the kitchen." And she practically prances out, looking very satisfied.

"Let's play." Bea demands. Cameron shakes his head at this, completely exasperated, and I stifle a smile.

"What do we do then?" Bea asks, jutting her chin out.

"Let's talk." I suggest. This is our exact conversation from two minutes ago. We're getting nowhere.

"I –" Cameron stutters, trying to make small talk, awkward as ever. "I mean, ma would be fine if you... ever wanted to come by the farm, you know. And, you know..."

I wring my hands.

"You know..." he continues. "Paul really is sorry. No, really. He's been a wreck."

"Alright," I say slowly, feeling Winnie's curious gaze on me. "Great." I regret saying that afterwards, but it's the only word I can think to respond with on the spot.

"Um," Bea chips in. Her mood has back flipped again; her eyes are mournful. "Janine?"

"Yeah?"

"It's about my gran."

I bite my lip worriedly. Next to me, Cameron shakes his head disapprovingly and Winnie leans in with interest.

"She… she really is a witch, like Winnie said," Bea says, so quietly that I'm not even sure if I heard her right.

"Hmm?" Cameron says, frowning, totally lost. Winnie smiles smugly, but stays silent.

"Shh," I tell Cam. "Bea, I'm sure that not true. Winnie… exaggerates a lot, you know… Don't you, Winnie? Don't take it to heart."

Winnie looks surprised and Bea shakes her head vigilantly. "No, but I know all the signs!" she insists. "Obviously, she's old and wrinkly. Winnie says that's–"

"A sure sign of a witch." Cameron and I cut in. We know this all off by heart.

"Hmm!" Winnie exclaims in approval, as if to say, *"Exactly!"*.

"And she's grown a massive wart on the side of her nose!"

"A sure sign of a witch." Cameron recites. I don't join in this time.

"Bea, there are *tonnes* of old ladies that aren't witches. And warts… they're just like spots. It doesn't really mean anything." I tell her earnestly, coming to my senses. Winnie has a clever way of winding people around her little finger to do and think exactly like she does, but she's not always right, after all. Bea isn't convinced though, and neither is suspicious Cameron.

"There's more, though, Janine," she persists. "She's even more ill now. I told Winnie about this, right? … And she says she must've cursed you because I went out without telling her, and now her powers are tired and everything." Winnie opens her mouth to agree, probably, but is cut off.

"Hey!" Cameron cries out, surprising all of us, I think. "That's so mean! Janine's not cursed!"

"It's what Winnie said," Bea says persistently.

"Wait," Winnie says gingerly, seeing how much that's upset Cameron.

Cameron can't seem to get his words out. "Yeah… well… Winnie doesn't know everything, alright?"

"She does. She knows about *witches*, and *magic*..."

"Well, she clearly doesn't know much about friends!" he blurts out. Winnie watches him, her expression frozen on her face and unreadable.

They're full-on arguing now. I'm about to break it up (and thank Cameron for his efforts), but Mum walks in just then.

"Are you all alright? I thought I heard shouting." She says. "Everything OK, Janine?" she whispers to me. I nod and smile at her, hoping she'd go so that we can sort all this out, but she holds out a plate of cookies.

"I made them," she says proudly. "Who wants to try?"

None of us makes a move. I think we're all thinking back to the spicy gingerbread day.

"Do these... have chilli in them?" Cameron asks, as politely as he can.

"No... no, they do not," she goes a bit pink, but laughs and makes for the door. "I'll be... right through here if you need me."

It's the third time she's said that. I think she's more nervous about my friends than I am.

There's a loud crunch. I look over to Bea to find her happily feasting on a cookie. "You should have one. Tell your ma they're really good." She tells me through a mouthful of crumbs.

There are a few seconds of silence. I catch Cameron looking at me, and he goes tomato-red. His ears blush too, like always.

"Tell us more about your grandma, Bea," I say, trying to break the ice a little. It's the wrong thing to say – Bea will get over-excited again and Cameron will get worked up, and I don't even believe any of this witch nonsense anyway, but I've said it now and Bea starts to talk animatedly.

"Like I said, she's really ill," she begins.

"Oh, not this again!" Cameron protests, throwing his hands in the air.

"Why are you being like this? I didn't say anything you weren't already thinking," Winnie says, frowning.

"Huh?" Bea ponders, lost.

"It's alright, Cameron," I whisper.

"...Yeah, so she's ill," Bea repeats. "And she's only staying in her bed. And she barely eats, and can't drink too much either. And we're all out of her medicine."

"It doesn't mean she's a witch if she's *sick*, Bea," I tell her.

"Yeah, that's not a sign of a witch." Cameron states.

"But there's more," Bea whimpers. I'm wondering if she's going to start making things up now.

"She says because she's ill, I'm not allowed to stay in her room with her for a long time," she says slowly. I don't know if this means that she's trying to remember or that she's trying to invent some wild story.

"Mhmm," I say appreciatively. I know that you're supposed to act like you believe small children's made-up stories. Next to me, Cameron rolls his eyes but stays silent. Winnie rolls her eyes too, but I don't think it's for the same reason.

"And there's been a black cat hanging around our house, you know," she finishes. At least, I hope she has.

"Ohhh," I say, like that's ultimately convinced me.

"Sure sign of a witch," Cameron mutters. I'm not sure if he's serious or not, but Bea seems pleased with our reactions. She smiles to herself for a few seconds.

"You know," she says, her cheeks stretched in her smile. "I've missed you, Janine. I mean," she stops, glancing at Winnie and Cameron. "You guys are great too. But Janine... you're always nice to me,"

I feel a bit bad now for not believing her, but I smile along with her anyway. "Thanks."

Cameron grunts. Winnie smiles unexpectedly.

"What?" I ask, surprised.

"I've missed you too. Obviously. We all have, I mean." Cameron says.

"You wouldn't believe how much we've missed you," Winnie adds, her eyes serious.

I muffle my laugh. "Um, yes. I've missed you all as well. Obviously."

"Janine," Bea interrupts. "I want to go home."

19

Bea

It hits me, the guilt that I've left Gran on her own. I have a bad feeling that I can't explain, but I know that it's time for me to go home. I don't mind that the rest of my friends will have fun without me. I need to go and take care of Gran.

"I want to go home," I tell Janine, hoping she'll understand. I regret telling them my doubts about her being a witch. I hate that I'm still so uncertain. I want to believe that Janine's right; that Winnie just got into my head. But it can't be true; she's just a sick old woman.

"Oh, don't be silly," Janine says gently. "Did Cam and Winnie upset you?"

"Sorry Bea, we didn't mean it," Cameron says on cue.

"No," I mumble, trying to think how to explain. "My gran's ill. I told you. I need to go home to take care of her,"

"Didn't you say she was resting?" Winnie chips in. "I'm sure she's fine, Bea," she reassures me kindly. I don't have time to appreciate her niceness right now.

"Janine, I need to go," I insist. She bites her lip.

"Are you sure? We'd love for you to stay for a bit longer,"

I consider everything again. Maybe Gran is fine at home. She does need the rest. Maybe she wants me to stay and enjoy myself with my friends. I push down my fears.

"Alright," I say happily. "Just a bit longer."

Janine smiles. I feel calm again. Then the door bursts open.

◄◆►

20

Winnie

I hear Janine's mother rush to answer it the door; then she calls my name.

"Winnie!"

"Winifred!" comes my mother's voice, shrill and scared. It's my parents. A few seconds later, the door slams open and Mother and Father stand there, stricken.

"I think something's wrong with the baby!" Mother says from the doorway, her voice trembling. "We're going to the hospital to check that everything's alright."

"What?" I exclaim. This can't be happening.

"You'll stay here at Janine's house until we return," Mother tells me, breathing deeply, looking troubled.

"No!" I cry. I can't stay here while my parents are at the hospital. I need to go too. I need to know what's happening. "I want to come with you!"

"Are you sure?" Mother asks. "Wouldn't you rather stay here with your friends?"

I think about it for no longer than a second.

"I want to come with you," I say again, gentler this time because I don't want to offend Janine's mother. I don't want to stay here anymore anyway; even though I don't mind Bea so much anymore, this whole witch thing was all being pinned onto me and I could feel them all becoming angry with me. Mother glances apologetically at Janine's mother.

"No, no, don't worry about it," she says reassuringly. "I hope everything's alright with the baby," Mother nods and smiles at her. Father takes Mother's hand hurriedly.

"Winifred, if you're coming, hurry up, your mother is in *pain!*" he says, not yelling but somehow having a huge effect all the same. In the duration of a minute, no one is laughing and talking and having fun anymore. I rush out, hardly even stopping to say goodbye to my friends. Mother hurriedly thanks Janine's mother for having me over. She's being civil and trying to contain herself, but I can see her screwing and unscrewing and wedding ring back and forth, on and off her finger, and I know that she feels anxious. Both of my parents are so tense and rattled by what's happening that I can't help but panic too. I don't want for there to be something wrong with the baby. Mother ushers me into a taxi waiting outside on the curb, then she carefully sits next to me in the back. Father sits in the front next to the driver and tells him to go to the hospital. The driver whistles quietly under his breath, and Father flashes him an annoyed glance, but he doesn't notice. Mother takes a deep breath and reaches for my hand and squeezes it. I try hard not to think about the last time I had to be driven somewhere – in August, when Paul dropped us off at the festival. The drive to there had been uneventful; tedious, even. Paul bickered with Cameron the whole time, and ignored me completely, except when he grinned at me at intervals in the rear view mirror each time he cracked a bad joke at Cameron's expense, peering expectantly, waiting for me to laugh along. Each time, I would turn away uncomfortably, and he would snort stupidly, unfazed. Before we knew it, though, we had arrived, and I remember clambering out hurriedly with Cameron, and the stuffy silence that settled as we waited for the others. This car journey seems to stretch out forever, though. My hand grows damp in Mother's. I wasn't paying attention, but I think the taxi driver asked Father a question; something trivial, small talk, really. No one replies to him, and the driver doesn't repeat the question. When we get to the hospital eventually, both my parents scramble out of the taxi and I rush after them. Father presses banknotes into the driver's outstretched palm. The sun is setting now, and everything is flooded in hot syrup. I hear the revving of the taxi's engine as it leaves. It all feels so strange. We burst into the hospital. Mother and I scurry inside as Father holds the grubby doors open. He quickly talks to the receptionist, who tells Mother to take a seat while she finds a doctor. I suddenly imagine Janine here, in her wheelchair, being cared for by the nurses, and her mother sitting on the cold seats that we are using now, enclosed between these dull walls. I wonder what was going through their heads.

"Ma'am!" a doctor calls, and Mother and Father and I stand and follow him into a different room. This room is brilliantly lit; cool white light washes over my skin. A bead of sweat on Father's temple is illuminated, and Mother's face looks sickly in the harsh glare. I realise that maybe I am a bit out of place here; maybe I should've stayed with Janine. Certainly, when I hover by the side of the door as the doctor talks to Mother and starts to examine her, I feel like I'm getting in the way. Mother's doctor must sense that I'm uncomfortable, because she asks if I'd like to step outside, back into the waiting room. I can't seem to get any coherent words out – Father ushers me out, while Mother stares after me, one hand rubbing her belly, frowning anxiously. I'm grateful to be able to leave, and I wait there until they all finish. I stare at the grey walls; the same grey walls that Janine and her mother must have seen a few months ago. Finally, my parents emerge, Father sweaty and Mother weary and relieved.

"False alarm," Mother tells me, smiling weakly.

21

Bea

After Winnie leaves, the mood changes and Janine and Cameron begin chatting casually. No one brings up Gran anymore. I remain on edge though, and no matter what I do, I can't stop thinking of her, sick, in bed, coughing. I know that I need to get home. I've had an awful feeling since I arrived at Janine's house. I can't wait any longer. I'll be sorry to have left and missed out on being with my friends, but at least I'll be home with Gran.

"Janine, I'm sorry but I really need to go home," I tell her earnestly when there's a break in her conversation with Cameron. She looks surprised but she's very considerate about it.

"Oh. We'd love for you to stay a bit longer, but I understand if you need to take care of your grandma," she says thoughtfully.

"It's getting kind of dark," Cameron observes. I look towards the window and realise he's right. It must be late. I really need to go to Gran. Janine bites her lip.

"It is… Will you be alright to go home by yourself?" she asks. I nod hurriedly.

"Yeah, I'll be fine, thanks," I say, smiling despite myself because I love that she's so caring. No one says anything for a few seconds.

"Well, I'll see you later then," Janine says.

"Bye!" I say, getting up from my seat and stooping down to her wheelchair to hug her. She's a bit taken aback, but then she relaxes and hugs me back.

"Calm down, she's in a wheelchair!" Cameron hisses. I take no notice and squeeze her for a few more seconds before letting go, because Janine seems to be fine.

"Bye!" I shout again by the door. "Tell your ma that those cookies were amazing."

I tried my best to be polite and friendly, but in reality, I'm becoming more and more worried. I should've left before, when there was still light outside. The sun is already down now, and everything is becoming more and more shadowy. I try to swallow down the fear and think of Gran, but that makes me even more anxious.

I don't have very long left until I reach my house. I'm almost there. I've almost reached Gran.

22

Janine

Bea slams the front door on her way out, and we hear a stir from the kitchen. Mum stumbles out, her eyes red and tired.

"I'm so sorry, I fell asleep... Where's Bea?" she mumbles drowsily.

"She had to leave, Mum," I explain.

"She said she really liked your cookies, by the way," Cameron adds.

"How lovely," Mum says, stretching. "Right. You guys need anything? Cameron, do let me know if you have to leave as well."

He nods obediently and Mum ushers out of the room again. "I'll be in here if you guys... you know the drill." She calls, trailing off.

"So," I say. It's just me and Cam now. "Did... did you really believe any of that about Bea's grandma being a witch?" he scoffs.

"No, of course not. She's making it up." he tells me, although I know that he had completely believed her at first. "I think her gran really is ill, though." he adds.

"Yes, I think so too," I agree. "Do you think she caught whatever her grandma has?" I blurt out.

"What?" he exclaims, so loudly that it surprises me.

"Sorry, I meant... the illness; I'm not talking about curses and magic and stuff anymore," I say, smiling. "No, seriously though – do you think Bea's alright?"

"I dunno. If her gran's a witch, probably not,"

I laugh. "Yeah, right. Her grandma's not a witch," I pause. "Right?"

"Well," he considers it. "Let's think about it. She's old, right?"

"Old and haggard," I quip before I can stop myself.

"And she recently grew a mole on her face," he continues. "She's weak and can't get out of bed, and took a turn for the worse since… your accident."

I wince at the word.

"…Sorry," he says uncomfortably.

"It's fine, really." I pause. "I know it sounds dumb, but I'd forgotten about it for a second."

He's silent for a moment. I know what he's thinking.

"No, I can't walk," I sigh. He looks deflated.

"Do you want–" he starts, then stops himself. He looks like he wants to be tactful.

"Um," I say, hesitating. We're both quiet. The silence feels prickly.

"I don't think I can walk, though, Cam," I mumble, my voice crackling. This isn't totally true; I've been refusing for a few weeks to even start trying, though I didn't ever suspect that I could actually do it.

He looks frustrated now, like he blames himself for bringing all this up. I try not to look like I'm about to cry, even though I feel like it.

There's another second of complete silence. I watch as his face reddens from embarrassment, then I suddenly demand: "Help me get up."

I'm just trying to seem confident and self-assured like I normally am. I don't know if he believes me though, because he suddenly looks a bit sad for me and his eyebrows arch up into his forehead. "Really?"

I nod, feeling a bit sick now: less sure of myself than I was before. I hold out my hand though, and he grabs it. He takes the other one too, for good measure, and using a bit of his force and a bit of mine, I lift into an upright position.

"This is good," he says. The excitement and apprehension and uncertainty of this major thing happening is in the air, but neither of us acknowledges it.

I try to smile, but my forehead is slick with sweat already. I don't quit though, because Cameron looks so glad that I'm doing this. I wouldn't have let Winnie help me like this, for pride, but it's alright if it's Cameron somehow, because he's so much more honest and relaxed.

"Do you want to take a step?" he asks in disbelief, like he can't quite believe that this is happening. I don't reply, mulling it over. "Only a small one," he tells me. "I'll hold your arm, so you won't fall." he whispers.

One white socked foot of mine moves forward – slowly, like a turtle. I know that I'm moving it, but it's all so surreal that it feels like someone else's foot. It crosses my mind then how we were talking about witches one second, and now I'm *walking*. My heart booms in my chest.

I stumble. In that moment, I look at Cameron and he looks defeated, thinking that's it, I'm giving up.

My other foot takes a step. Now, I realise excitedly, I'm few good inches away from the wheelchair.

The process repeats. Left foot, right foot, stop. I'm holding on to his arm so hard that the blood is squeezed out, leaving faded yellow fingerprints imprinted on his skin. He glances at me quickly. I sense it and get startled, but I force a hard smile. I'm doing great. I know I am.

Just then, I lose my balance. It's ironic, really: just when I realised that I could actually sort of walk again, I got distracted and tripped over my own feet.

Cameron isn't quick enough, and I clumsily drop onto the floor. The way his face contorts in terror at this almost makes me laugh, but I'm not hurt – the carpet is plush, and I landed fairly tidily. I'm not in a worse state than I was before, in any case.

"Are you alright? Can you move? Does it hurt?" Cameron gabbles worriedly.

"I'm fine, really!"

"Do you want me to call your ma? Do you want to go to the hospital? Does it hurt?" he parrots mindlessly, his eyes wide in fright.

"I said I'm fine, Cam. I just *fell*. Help me get up."

He hurriedly grips onto one of my arms, so tightly I'm worried it'll leave my skin bruised, but I just thank him because he looks nauseated enough to pass out anyway. Somehow, though, he gets his shaky legs to cooperate and he eases me surprisingly smoothly back into my wheelchair.

"I'm so sorry." He breathes, placing his hands underneath his legs as he sits down to stop them from trembling. "Are you alright?" he turns swiftly to me again. "Does it hurt?" he repeats for the thousandth time.

"Cameron, it's fine," I tell him, trying to laugh to lighten the mood. His bottom lip quivers, like he's about to cry.

"A-alright." Cameron says. He sounds like he's trying to reassure me, or maybe himself. "Hey, you were doing really well though," His voice is brighter already, and I smile. Then he says,

"What if she's really a witch though?"

My shoulders droop, deflated, and I frown. Considerate and sweet as Cameron may be sometimes, he can also be so childish.

"I thought we decided that she isn't." I complain.

He moves his hands around to gesture, animated under the dim light. "You never know, though, right? I told you about that mole, didn't it? That's a sure sign of a witch."

"What if there aren't any signs? What if there aren't any witches?" I cut in.

"But what if there are? Bea's gran would be one for sure!" Cameron cries excitedly. He quickly clears his throat and regains his composure.

"Calm down," I giggle. He looks at me and laughs along, but we're both still thinking about our conversation.

"What if she's testing her spells on Bea?" he blurts out suddenly.

I scoff. "That's ridiculous."

"Maybe. But..." he continues, leaving his sentence hanging, trying to be mysterious. I roll my eyes.

"Stop, Cameron,"

He shakes his head cunningly, and I almost burst out laughing.

"Well, she – Bea's gran, I mean – isn't exactly normal anyway, is she?" he says insistently.

"She–" I try to explain.

"I mean, all of this hiding inside all day..." he persists.

"She's ill, remember?"

"Is she?" he queries, looking so sceptical that I can't help but be amused.

"She's just a poor old woman, Cameron," I remind him.

"I know," he sighs. We're both quiet for a moment.

He's looking at the ground now. I'm glad that I convinced to stop having doubts about Mrs Anderson, but I think about what he's been saying. Maybe I'm being childish now, but I start to grow anxious as I think about the possibility of him being right.

"... So she's old." I state. Cameron's gaze flickers up to me, surprised.

"A sure sign of a witch." he says.

"And she looks ugly." I say. It sounds kind of mean after I've said it, but Cameron leaps on the chance to repeat his favourite line:

"A sure sign of a witch!"

"...Like, with moles and warts and everything." I add for good measure.

"A sure sign of a–"

"Yeah, yeah, I know!" I laugh.

"Oh, and the black cats that hang around their house!" Cameron bursts out. I grin and nod quickly, but I can't remember if that's actually true or not.

There's a pause, during which neither of us speaks. The excitement of our conversation hovers expectantly in the air.

"So she's a witch." Cameron says. I don't really know if it was meant as a question or not, but I sort of nod in agreement, although I still have some clouded doubts, and I'm not quite sure how we came to this conclusion.

"Do you think... do you think it's safe for Bea to be living with her?" Cameron asks me quietly. That brings me to my senses.

"I don't know." I reply worriedly. My eyebrows knit together. My head spins with wild images of curses and evil spells, and vulnerable Bea at home in her cottage.

"Maybe we could check on her." he suggests.

Without thinking, I exclaim loudly,

"Yes!"

And I don't even have time to stop and think before Cameron leaps up, struggles to get my wheelchair outside and we're gone.

I hadn't realised how dark it had gotten since the sun went down. It seems even darker than when Bea left. The sky looks grey and smudged with traces of clouds that float along like phantoms. The air seems bitingly cold. Apart from the odd *whoosh*ing of a brutal gust of wind, it's eerily silent.

However, unfazed, Cameron and I set on our journey. I don't even consider Mum and how distraught she would be to find us disappeared.

Cameron pushes my wheelchair along the gritty ground. He's trying to go too fast. It's making me jitter uncomfortably in my seat, and he's tiring himself out too. I can hear him holding his breath a bit so that I can't hear him panting. I don't say anything though.

Bea's house feels miles away. It's only down the road, but the journey feels lengthy and exhausting. At first, I long to get there sooner, but the nearer we get, the more uncertain I become about this.

Cameron says nothing. The silence is a bit scary.

My fingers feel stiff and sore from the cold. I think of Mum suddenly, as we approach the cottage. What if she's woken up? It's too late to go back now, anyway, but I wish we could.

I gulp.

"Cameron?"

"Hmm?" we come to a dead stop in front of the door.

"C-could we go b–"

"Wait, *shh*!"

I frown but listen to him. "What?" I whisper.

"Can't you hear it?" he hisses back, standing next to me.

"No!" I reply, close to tears. I'm not even sure why. I'm scared.

Then I do hear it. A muffled wailing is coming from inside the cottage. My skin prickles all over and my head feels light as air. Looking over at Cameron, I see his pallid face.

"Is that the witch?" I whisper.

"I think it's Bea." Cameron says. I'm hit with a blow of relief, which is strange, seeing as Bea is crying, but it makes me feel safer.

"We should knock. We should see if she's alright." I state, with newly found liveliness.

Cameron looks at me like I'm crazy, but he knocks. Bea creaks open the door. Slowly, her face is revealed in the dimming light. Her hair is dishevelled; her eyes are red and puffy; her shaking hands are held over her mouth as she sobs.

"Bea!" I exclaim. "What happened?"

"It's Gran," she says, weeping.

"What did she do to you?" Cameron demands.

"She… nothing, she…" Bea says in-between small hiccups. "She… died."

The tears fall faster and heavier than before now, and Bea's chest is heaving with every breath, but she attempts to keep talking.

"She… she'd been ill for a long– … long time, a-and now she… she died."

I feel like someone's puncturing holes in my chest. I sort of wish she'd stop talking, but of course it's impossible. Next to me, Cameron is in shock, all pale and wide-eyed.

"I-I think she didn't… didn't want m-me to… stay in her room so I d-didn't… see …" Bea groans, like it physically hurts her, and she can't carry on.

"You can't stay here," I say. "Don't worry. You can come home with me. It's alright. Don't worry. My mum can sort everything out. Don't worry."

"Yeah, yeah, don't worry," Cameron adds, placing a hand on my wheelchair armrest. I think it was to steady himself. He doesn't look any steadier, though.

"Thank you," Bea says, trying to get her breath back.

"Here, look, calm down," I implore her desperately. I grab her hands and squeeze them in mine and breathe slowly. She mimics, and soon she isn't crying that hard anymore. Her cheeks are still tomato-red, and she looks exhausted, but she can breathe now.

"My gran was my last living family." She mumbles after a few quiet seconds.

"I'm sorry," I say. I feel guilty and horrible: guilty for thinking of poor Mrs Anderson as a witch, horrible for not being able to do anything to help Bea. Actually, just pure horrible. Horrible about *everything*.

"I'm sorry too." Cameron says earnestly. His head is bowed down and he's looking seriously at the floor, like he's praying at church. I remember suddenly my visit there with Mum, and try desperately to recall some of the things that the priest said.

"She's in a better place, Bea," I tell her quietly.

"I bet she's in heaven," Cameron adds shakily, trying to be supportive.

"Let's go home, Bea." I say after a silent pause.

We all go back to my house, Bea trudging a few paces ahead of us melancholically and Cameron wheeling me behind her. The sky is darker than ever now. Wisps blacken over foggy stars. The whole sky looks mournful. And actually, we're in a pretty mournful mood too.

"So… she wasn't a witch." Cameron says, too quiet for Bea to hear. He sighs, and I sigh too.

"No. I feel so bad."

"Me too. Trust me."

There's a silence. We're both deep in thought. The wheelchair rattles as it bumps over grit and gravel.

I look around at the sky again, at how sad this whole scene is. It all envelopes us, like a soft blanket. I can't breathe under it.

I think of Mum back at home, and how she might react. I think of Winnie, and how we'll ever explain all of this to her when we see her again. I think of how meaningless the idea of school is now. I look at the sky, and it's all so *sad*.

Something catches my eye then. A glint; a magic silver moonbeam. The moon is full, flourished, grinning down at us.

"Cam!" I call. But he's already looking as well.

"The full moon, that's the most magical kind of moon," he tells me in a hushed voice. I don't argue with him. It is.

There's a harsh yowl behind us. We both look quickly, and sure enough, a dozen cats with ink-dark fur have gathered around the cottage door.

Looking back at Cameron, I realise that he's thinking the same thing. It doesn't even matter anymore. It doesn't mean anything anymore. A poor old woman died. We need to take care of Bea now.

Part 3

1

Cameron

Paul stays at home now. He doesn't go up to the city anymore. Ma was so pleased when he returned for good that she baked him pies and cakes for weeks, and fussed over him like a baby. Pa pretended to be moody and grumpy and indifferent, but they've been spending heaps of time together. Pa has been teaching him how to take care of the farm. Paul doesn't really care for the animals, he leaves most of that to me, but he gets so funnily excitable when Pa goes driving in his tractor with him that I don't even mind.

It was because of me that Paul stopped seeing his friends in the city. He took me over there, at the beginning of this summer after school broke up – and it wasn't fun at all. They were awful. Paul showed me all the bars he used to hang around, all the boys he used to get into trouble with. Some weren't as friendly as he remembered. A couple of them found me on my own, utterly lost and defenceless without Paul, and picked on me a little. They didn't beat me up badly, just teased me really, but when Paul found out, something seemed to snap in him. He ran after them – turned the corner and went after them. He was gone for several minutes; I don't know what happened, but Paul came back unscathed and after that we went straight back home to the farm. He didn't tell our parents about it. He didn't even tell me what happened properly. He just said that he wasn't ever going back to them. I guess he still felt bad about it though, because a week later he sold his shiny red car and bought us both mountain bikes. Pa grieved after it, but Paul was glad to be rid of it. He hadn't driven it since Janine's accident.

We go riding on our bikes together sometimes. We talk too – at first it was so strange, because Paul never really paid much attention to me, but now I think he really cares. It's like my brother was completely reborn. No one talks about it, but he hasn't drunk in months. More than anyone else, the accident horrified him because he was responsible, and I think that guilt will stay with him forever. I don't blame him anymore though; at least, I'm not angry with him. He's making an effort to change.

We're riding our bikes together right now.

"Aren't you bored?" I ask him. The sun is setting and the countryside is a golden green blur around us.

"Bored? Of what? This is fun!" Paul bellows back, loud and showy as ever.

"Bored of home!" I yell back as we enter a thicket and bushes block our vision slightly.

"What? Mate, the city was pretty boring too... I didn't really do anything all day..." he pauses and swerves to a stop. "Cam! Wait a minute, I'm out of breath." And we exit the thicket and come into a vast grassy opening.

"I'm not," I say, grinning, but I halt next to him.

"Isn't that Janine?" he says after a minute or two. I look and there she is, struggling up the hill to the farm, pink in the face, her expression set hard with determination. She hasn't seen us.

"Race you!" Paul shouts suddenly, and speeds off on his bike before I can react. I follow quickly, laughing and panting and suddenly boiling hot in the humid summer air.

2

Bea

I love my home. It's different to living with Gran... so different. We ate cherries from the cherry tree a couple of months ago, when it bloomed. They were lovely.

Everything is filled with light. When the sun comes up in the morning, it seems to choose this house first, and all the rooms are flooded with its rays, the curtains bursting and barely able to contain it. On week days I help Gina with breakfast and some of the cleaning. She doesn't ask me to, but I'm so accustomed to doing this that it comes naturally. On weekends we do gardening together. Janine doesn't like to get her hands dirty, so she often sits on a bench, watching us, scowling in the sun, wearing Cameron's floppy sun hat. I don't know if he gave it to her or if she just took it from him.

Every morning, Gina lets us wake up late and have long, relaxed breakfasts and go out to meet with our friends. We all three of us sit at the table and eat together. Both of them are quite sullen and irritable in the mornings, so I do a lot of the talking. Then Janine and I go out to play, normally. Janine doesn't need her wheelchair anymore. She's so much happier without it – nowadays, she uses crutches. Though she's moody in the mornings, she often perks up, which always puts me more at ease. She likes to go on walks; I like them too, and I always start pointing out interesting this as we pass them by – a butterfly, a large noisy bird, a broken television dumped by the side of the road. Janine isn't very patient sometimes, and dismisses my observations, but I know she doesn't really find me annoying because other times she joins in and we make a whole game of it. By the afternoon, she's much cheerier, especially when we meet with Winnie and Cameron. I never used to like other children, I used to find them quite menacing and intimidating, but now I have friends and they're nothing like that. Winnie was a bit mean at first, but even she is lovely now.

It's nothing like my life before.

3

Winnie

He cries all the time, my little brother. He's fat and beaming and toothless, with glowing skin and enormous brown eyes. Father melts just looking at him. Mother has been exhausted, but happier, I think. I've been happier too. But he just seems to cry, and cry, and cry. At first it was almost unbearable, but now I feel ever so grown-up because Mother showed me how to hold him properly, and when I hug him closely, he stops crying at once. I know how to burp him, and change his nappy. He doesn't eat proper food yet, but when Mother isn't feeding him, I can even give him milk from a little baby bottle. I hold him and watch him suckle on it. When he's tired, I gently rock him and he clutches at my fingers and is lulled to sleep. When he cries, it's irritating, but when he's cheerful and jolly, it sort of fills me up with happiness. Everyone runs around the house doing whatever he needs, but I don't mind it; he's so small and cute that it doesn't matter that he's in the centre of attention. The first time that all my friends met him, I held him proudly as they giggled and played with him, and Mother watched contentedly from the side. I let Janine try to hold him too, but he became so wriggly that I took him straight back. Bea wanted to as well, but I didn't let her. I didn't let anyone else hold him again after that. I'm petrified that they'll drop him and he'll get hurt. I don't ever want him to be in pain.

Sometimes, in the morning, I wake up early and creep into his baby room, being careful not to wake up Mother and Father in the adjacent room. If I'm accidentally too loud, his big eyes snap open and watch me inquisitively as a tower over his cot. He almost never cries when I wake him up. I sometimes pick him up and play with him until Mother wakes up. At first, I didn't even want to go to school after he was born, because I didn't want to be away from him. I never get tired of him though. I never get angry with him either. It seems Father has been much calmer since he was born too. It's having the best effect on us as a family.

4

Janine

Everything has changed since last summer. For a start, I don't use a wheelchair anymore. I'm still a bit unsteady sometimes, so I have to use crutches and I kind of hobble around everywhere, but it's a huge improvement and I was over the moon when the doctors told me.

Secondly, Bea moved in with me and Mum. It was so odd at first. I wanted the best for her, which was why I suggested the idea in the first place, though Mum was a bit more reluctant. Bea seemed to lose her spirit for a while after her grandma died. She was miserable, but I didn't know how to help. I was still adjusting too, but now I'm so glad to have her living with us. She fits with us in ways we couldn't have imagined: she loves baking and gardening with Mum, but also playing and messing about with me. Mum adores her, and I do too, more than ever before. They've been trying loads of cake recipes together, because the summer festival is in a couple of weeks and Mum's determined to win the prize for best cake this year. Last year, the prize was a set of antique teacups; this year, it's rumoured that it's a dining table and chairs set. Mum says she wants a change from some of Great-Uncle Casper's stuffy furniture.

The remainder of the school year after my accident was a struggle, in some ways. The school wasn't very good at accommodating wheelchairs, or even giving sufficient space for my crutches sometimes after I started using them. If I hadn't had my friends with me, I would've just quit, but they were all so encouraging that I almost couldn't bear to let them down, even though it wasn't even about them. I saw that it was difficult for them too – at one point, Winnie's and Bea's relationship became seriously strained, worse than it had been before. Maybe it was something to do with the fact that Bea was living with us now.

Cam remained sweet and kind as ever, and he put away any doubts about Mrs Anderson being a witch immediately after we found out she'd died.

I've been thinking about Paul, and I don't blame him anymore for what happened. It was wrong to pin everything on him; it all started with me being careless. It's all turning out OK now. It's fine – I know I'm going to be fine.

One silly thing that never got resolved, in my mind, was seeing Dolly again. Cameron would tell me all about the farm, but I never got to see her again after that first time on the road as we were arriving here one year ago. Partly because trekking up a frozen hill in the winter would've been a pain for me. But now, here I am, my knees shaking, pushing myself to climb up to the farm. I didn't let Mum come with me to help; I want to do this myself. I have to stop though. I look around and the setting sun, at the quaint farmhouse on the grassy mound. I hope Cameron's at home. This might be a bit awkward if he isn't. He promised that he'd take me to see Dolly again though.

I get to the farmhouse, panting and hot in the face. Instantly, I'm startled by a flurry of figures that whizz past me so quickly that I'm almost knocked to the floor.

"Hey!" I exclaim. I look back to see Cameron and Paul, braking their bikes, laughing.

Cam and Paul take me to see Dolly. The path is bumpy and difficult, but I manage it. Dolly is grazing distantly, but as soon as she sees her owners, she ambles towards us by the fence. Closer up, I notice things about her that I'd forgotten: her short cropped black-and-white coat, her enormous head, her deep liquid eyes, her smell. Cam leads her into a barn for the night, where she quickly settles down because this is familiar to her, this is her home. Then he locks it up and all three of us head back up.

"I'm sorry," Paul murmurs. It's almost dark now.

I glance up at him. I don't know what to say, so I just smile and hope he gets it. He does. He smiles back.

◆

5

Bea

A cat yowls loudly as I pass him by; he scurries into a hedge. I think I might cry. I haven't been here since the funeral. It's late; so dark, but oddly warm, as if someone's hot breath is on my skin, as if I'm swaddled in the humidity like a baby.

The graveyard is dreary and traditional: a bland, grassy area punctured with dry, bald, well-trodden spots. There's a bin, right beside the entrance gates, filled with dead, withered flowers. I force myself to keep walking, though the closer I get, the weaker my knees are and the sicker I feel. I don't have long – I promised Gina I'd be back soon.

I reach it at last; Gran's grave. I lay down the flowers that Gina got as delicately as I can, my hands shaking. I gulp and breathe deeply.

Everything is still. I can hear my own ragged breathing and Gina speaking on the phone outside the graveyard distantly. Apart from this, it's silent.

After a couple of minutes, I return, feeling a little wobbly but pleased that I'd done it. Sure enough, Gina is waiting patiently with Janine. I'm surprised when Janine rushes up to me and hugs me.

"I didn't know you'd go through with it, Bea," she says earnestly.

"We're very proud," Gina says. I don't say anything. I think I might cry. I'm not alone.